JUSTIN CASE
Rules, Tools, and Maybe a Bully

JUSTIN CASE

Rules, Tools,
and Maybe a Bully

By **Rachel Vail**

Illustrated by **Matthew Cordell**

FEIWEL AND FRIENDS
New York

A FEIWEL AND FRIENDS BOOK
An Imprint of Macmillan

Feiwel and Friends books may be purchased for business or promotional use.
For information on bulk purchases, please contact the Macmillan Corporate
and Premium Sales Department at (800) 221-7945 x5442 or by e-mail at
specialmarkets@macmillan.com

Library of Congress Cataloging-in-Publication Data Available
ISBN: 978-1-250-03978-1 (hardcover) / 978-1-250-06194-2 (eBook)

Book design by Barbara Grzeslo/Véronique Lefèvre Sweet

Feiwel and Friends logo designed by Filomena Tuosto

First Edition: 2014

1 3 5 7 9 10 8 6 4 2

mackids.com

To my dad, who loves as full-heartedly as he lives and laughs.
Your little girl still thinks you hung the moon.—R.V.

For Dean—M.C.

September 1, Wednesday

I figured it out before I even opened my eyes.

I was half awake but still lying still, wondering why it felt like in my heart there was a kind of fighting.

And then, suddenly, my eyes opened because I knew:

September.

It was back.

September 2, Thursday

In our family we have a lot of rules. Like *Share*. That's a biggie.

But now it turns out that *Don't take Dad's stuff* is an even bigger one.

So after the yelling by Mom, I was not allowed to use Dad's tools anymore. Even though I really needed to build a lock to keep my little sister, Elizabeth, out of my room while Cash was over. Boys who are going into fourth grade don't need an almost first-grader barging in and saying we are playing too rough.

Even if we are.

Building something with a toolbox, I was thinking, might be a way to calm things down, for goodness sake, which is another rule in our family: *Not so wild in the house.*

We also have the *Please* and *Thank you* thing going strong here, and you're supposed to just remember to say them without even a hint. After you eat, you have to say *May I be excused?* and then clear your plate. Those are not rules in my second-best-friend Noah's family. Noah can just leave his stuff on the table and get up whenever he's done. I am not sure what the rule is in Cash's family, because they just moved here from Tennessee in June and I didn't even know we were such great friends during camp.

The way I found out we were such great friends in camp was: He told his mom we were, and so he wanted to have a playdate with me, so she called my mom on the phone with the news.

Nobody asked me if I wanted a playdate with Cash. My mom just said, *Of course, how wonderful, we'd be happy to have him over, how about Thursday?* so here he was. Today. Whacking my stuffties, even the olds and the fragiles, with my Nerf sword and smiling and saying what a great time we were having.

I said the word *yeah* to that. Because everybody says *yeah* to Cash. You can't help it.

No matter what Wingnut and Snakey think.

I wasn't being mean about their whacked and crumpled states. It's just impossible to disagree with Cash. Even when you actually do disagree.

When Cash first got dropped off, he told my mom he was pleased to meet her and thanked her for having him over at our beautiful home. I don't know if our home actually is beautiful or if that's just what people from Tennessee say instead of hello. My friends from here barely say hi and bye to parents.

Now probably some new rules are going to pop up in our family about what I have to say to people's parents about if their homes are beautiful.

—*mm*—

September 3, Friday

In our family you are not allowed to say the word *hate* even if you actually, you know, the-opposite-of-like something. You have to say *no thank you*. I am not sure why. Rules are not always explained in our family.

Things I *no, thank you*:

1. Trying on a billion new sneakers at the shoe store today and ending up with the shiny silver ones instead of the soft brown-without-laces ones.

2. Rules.

3. Rough stuff.

4. Bananas that are starting to get freckles.

—*mm*—

September 4, Saturday

What I should be doing today:

Getting ready for school to start, which it is going to do on Wednesday even though it's still Augusty hot.

What I am doing instead:

Going to the County Fair, where there will be pigs and pies and lumberjacks.

I didn't know we liked any of those things. I didn't even know we had a County. I thought we had a Town.

I am not a huge fan of surprises or the word *hurry*.

Or pie. Pie is fruit and goo, ganging up together and pretending to be dessert.

Dad showed me a newspaper article to prove how fun the County Fair would be. It said the lumberjacks throw axes.

I am not sure why Dad wants his kids near flying axes, but I am now pretending to have a Good Attitude just in case Dad is secretly evil.

mm

September 5, Sunday

Lumberjacks are awesome.

The one Elizabeth and I decided to root for was Mike

O'Sullivan. He came in second in sawing through a tree trunk (3.1 seconds) and first in chopping the top half of a log off the bottom half (7.3 seconds). He also got first prize in tossing an ax at a target to slice open the can of soda that is squooshed into the bull's-eye.

That is an actual event: throw an ax at a target and explode a soda.

I am totally going to be a lumberjack when I grow up, or at least for Halloween. Cash is too. He was also there, also rooting for Mike O'Sullivan.

Mike O' Sullivan

I am still not a fan of pie.

But it turns out I do like kettle corn, fried dough, foot-long hot dogs, watermelon wedges, and cotton candy. Also: County Fairs and newborn piglets.

And, best of all, not puking.

Elizabeth likes all the same stuff I do. Unfortunately, she did not get to enjoy the Not Puking part of the night.

—

September 6, Monday

Today is Labor Day. Usually we go to my grandparents'
condo at the beach for Labor Day. But this year Gingy and
Poopsie went on a cruise. If they like it, we can go on a cruise
with them next year, Poopsie promised. They called from their
first night on the ship to say that Poopsie forgot to pack any
pants.

Which I guess means that for the whole five days, Poopsie
has been running all around a boat in the middle of the ocean—
in his underpants. I totally want to go on a cruise like that.
Instead we went to the town pool.

We went with my second-best-friend, Noah, and his parents. Noah is a lot of fun, especially if you are interested in hearing about diseases.

Xavier Schwartz and Gianni Schicci were already at the pool when we got there. They called out my name—well, not my actual name, which is Justin Krzeszewski, because nobody can pronounce that last name right, including most of the people who have it hanging off the back of their regular name. The name they called was "Justin Case." Which is what everybody calls me. Well, everybody except grown-ups and Noah. Noah and grown-ups just call me Justin.

"Justin Case!" Xavier yelled. He was in midair. A second later he slammed into the pool with a huge splashing cannonball.

Gianni Schicci was waving both of his arms at me. "Justin Case! The Cannonball Champion of the World! Come on!"

I was the gold-medal winner in one thing at camp and that one thing was Cannonball. Cannonball is not an Olympic sport yet, but maybe it will be by the time I'm old enough.

I ran over and cannonballed into the pool. Me and Gianni and Xavier and then Cash, when he got there, all had a very splashy time until the lifeguard made us stop.

We decided to go get Popsicles at the snack bar.

Noah didn't come with us. He was still dry, sitting on the lounge chair between the moms, covered in towels to keep from getting a sunburn. He said he wasn't in the mood for Popsicles. So I said, "Okay," and ran over to catch up with Cash, Xavier, and Gianni.

It was the first time Noah ever wasn't in the mood for food.

I hope he is not getting a disease.

September 7, Tuesday

School starts tomorrow. My pencils are sharpened. My hair is cut. My new sneakers are bought.

So I guess I am ready.

My new sneakers were so ready, they were practically glowing in the dark. That is why my dog, Qwerty, chewed them up. Because probably he thought they were dangerous bad-guy glow-in-the-dark aliens invading our house and he wanted to protect us from them. Mom didn't get it. She had a very loud chat with him about inappropriate snacks.

It was not the first Mom-Qwerty chat on that topic.

Qwerty looked very sorry and ashamed.

I took him out to the backyard and secretly thanked him. Those darn sneakers were too shiny, as shiny as Bartholomew Wiggins. Bartholomew Wiggins wears a jacket and tie and puts gel in his hair every first day of school. And sometimes on random Fridays or when there's a class trip. He is the shiniest kid in my grade.

It's okay when first-graders look all shiny on the first day of school. But we are starting fourth grade, not first. Mom does not understand about sneakers looking better and more relaxed if they don't shine. Maybe fourth grade was different way back when she was in it. They didn't have computers or phones or music then either, I think, so maybe they had to make up for that by glowing in their sneakers.

My grandfather, Poopsie, didn't even have sneakers back when he was a kid. They weren't *invented*. And he had to walk uphill five miles to get to school, and then five miles uphill coming home, in the snow all year long.

Poopsie's stories don't always make a tremendous amount of sense. He says things were less settled back in The Day, which is when he grew up. That's why he kept walking uphill in every direction, barefoot.

He also had to play Stickball instead of normal games, and use a rock to get onto the Internet.

Anyway, Qwerty got very excited about that secret that I told him about liking his improvement of my sneakers. We jumped around, both very happy, until one of us got knocked down and covered with drool, and the other of us couldn't stop barking.

Then we decided to come in and calm down for goodness sake.

It is probably not that weird for a fourth-grader to be slightly worried before the first day of school. Even a little bit of worry can keep a person from falling asleep at bedtime. It doesn't mean the fourth-grader is still a worried kid just because he needs to hold on to his stuffties and wish that the summer could last a little while longer.

It probably doesn't mean I am an evil bad guy if I wish that maybe an earthquake would swallow up the school (not hurting anybody because it could happen in the middle of the night when nobody is in the school) so there would have to be a summer vacation extension until they could pull the school out of that deep hole.

Maybe using excavators and backhoes.

That would be cool.

Teachers probably get worried a little the night before the first day of school too. I think I heard about that as a fact somewhere. I bet from Noah. He knows billions of facts.

Fourth-grade teachers who are taller than your dad and can move their eyebrows independently of each other in a way that is maybe a code that the students better learn right away so they don't get in trouble, and who speak very quietly all the time and are named Mr. Leonard—even teachers like that might get a little worried the night before school starts.

But probably not.

Even my nicest stuffties like Wingnut and Really Giraffe don't think Mr. Leonard is spending tonight wishing his mom would come sing him an extra lullaby and maybe bring him an ice pack so his hot pillow would cool the heck down.

―――

September 8, Wednesday

I am officially a fourth-grader now.

I sure hope Mr. Leonard was interested in hearing about lumberjacks as a writing sample.

I am so used up, I can't even think.

―――

September 9, Thursday

There are a lot of transitions in fourth grade.

Mr. Leonard expects us to cope with transitions smoothly.

He calls us "young man" or "young lady" instead of our names. That's a transition, I think. Okay, I am not actually 100 percent sure what a transition is. But teachers in the lower grades say your name.

There's no complaining or whining in fourth grade. There is just *Clean up your stuff* and *Get in line.* Single file. Not a boys' line and a girls' line. We are too grown up for that, Mr. Leonard thinks. I am not sure he is correct on that one. But I didn't raise my hand to say, *Mr. Leonard, I am not sure you are correct about that one.*

No way. And neither did anybody else.

Mr. Leonard's voice is quiet and his face is very serious. Nobody looks out windows or falls off chairs while he talks, not even Xavier Schwartz, who is King of Falling Off Chairs.

And nobody says, *You're wrong, Mr. Leonard.* I bet ever. Probably not even his mom says that.

It is so weird to think maybe teachers have moms somewhere.

"Move silently through the corridors like a shark," Mr. Leonard was saying. Sharks are predators, I thought. I imagined myself as a shark chasing after a school (hahahaha) of little screaming kindergarteners.

But I wasn't a shark hunting anything. I was just Justin, sitting in my seat, smiling about eating kindergarteners with my multiple rows of shark teeth, while Mr. Leonard waited, looking at me.

I stopped smiling. I stopped imagining myself as a shark closing in on crying but cute, scared kindergartener-goldfish. I started concentrating on not crying like a scared kindergartener myself.

When I could listen again, Mr. Leonard was saying, "We have a lot to get through this year, including standardized fourth-grade tests." Fourth-grade tests count, Mr. Leonard explained. So there is no time to waste on rough transitions.

―――

September 10, Friday

Elizabeth *loves* first grade.

I *like* fourth grade.

Even if we have to use transition words in fourth grade, which, it turns out, almost nobody knew what they were before today. Xavier Schwartz raised his hand and asked if transition words were words like *cars* and *trains*.

Mr. Leonard smiled. "I think we'd call those transportation words, right, young man?"

Xavier nodded and stayed in his chair. In third grade he definitely would have been splattered all over the floor from that.

Mr. Leonard asked who could define transition words for the class. Montana C. could. She said they are just stuff like *for example*, *sometimes*, *also*, and *another thing* and *however*. She counted them out on her five right-hand fingers.

Everybody had to write those good transition words down in our notebooks. "They are tools in our toolbox," Mr. Leonard said.

Tools in our toolbox, I was thinking. So if Dad tries to say *for example*, for example, I can say, *Hey, Dad—no taking other people's tools out of their toolboxes!*

I was smiling, thinking that. Elizabeth better never say *also* ever again, because no taking other people's tools!

Then I looked up, and Mr. Leonard was watching me. I stopped smiling very fast. Again. Only the third day of school and already I was Looked At by the Teacher. TWICE.

For smiling. Both times.

All you could hear for a while was the scritch of new pencils on new notebook paper. When everybody finished writing down our transition words, Mr. Leonard said we should use those good new tools in sentences tonight, with underlines, for our homework.

Sometimes I really *no thank you* Montana C.

Also tools.

I am supposedly doing my homework now, sitting at my new desk that Dad put together for me with the actual tools from his toolbox. I am a fourth-grader now, he said, so I need my own desk to sit at and concentrate.

What I am doing instead of concentrating on homework while I sit here, though, is thinking about, *What if Mr. Leonard has this same desk in his room at his house and what if a screw needs tightening in Mr. Leonard's desk because his is a little wobbly like mine is and what if he tried to tighten the screw with a* sometimes?

Hahahaha. But I have to practice not smiling.

Justin K., 4-L Homework (3 Sentences about Fourth-Grade Positives)

1. Some things I like about fourth grade include *for example*: We have recess on the Upper Playground and *also* we have responsibility for the aquatic animals in the science lab. (Two transition words in that one!)

2. *Another thing* I enjoy is that instead of Chorus, we get recorders.

3. Even though I do not know *however* to play that squeaky thing.

—*ww*—

September 11, Saturday

I was waiting in line for my soccer jersey, trying to think of a good name for our team to go with our red-and-white striped jerseys. The players always get to vote on a team name, and I wanted to be the one with a good idea this year, for a change.

The Raspberry Swirls?

The Peppermint Sticks?

Urgh, all my ideas were so terrible.

The Blobs of Jam Swirled into Yogurts?

Yeah, all the other teams would really fear us.

I heard *Justin Case! Justin Case?* like it was coming from far away. When I looked up, Cash was signaling to me to come toward the front of the line where he was.

"I don't . . . " I started to answer.

The mom with the clipboard planted herself right in front of me and said right in my face: *Shhh!* Like I was rowdy or a troublemaker. When all I said was *I don't . . .* after Cash had been yelling out my 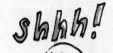 name so many times. I looked down quietly at my still slightly shiny sneakers.

But after a minute, when the Clipboard Mom walked to the front to see if there were any larger size shirts because Sam Pasternak grew a lot over the summer, Cash started calling my name again.

This time instead of starting to say, *I don't think I should come to where you are because that would be cutting the line,* I dashed up to where he was. He let me have the spot ahead of him.

And nobody put me in trouble for that.

Sometimes I fully don't get the rules at all.

―――

September 12, Sunday

I had to go to Elizabeth's soccer game this morning. Montana C. was there too, since her younger brother, Buckey, is on Elizabeth's team, The Purple Swizzles. Elizabeth had had the winning name choice for her team. My team ended up being The Flash. Cash suggested it, and since everybody says *yeah* to Cash, that was that. Luckily The Flash is a pretty cool name, probably better than The Blobs of Jam in Yogurts, at least. Or even The Purple Swizzles.

Montana C. poked me in the side with her elbow while I was thinking about team names. "What?" I asked, hoping I hadn't said *The Blobs of Jam in Yogurts* out loud.

She pointed at the field. I looked. Elizabeth and Buckey were running around in circles at midfield.

"What are they doing?" Montana C. whispered to me.

I shrugged.

Elizabeth and Buckey crashed into each other and fell down and then just stayed there plucking grass and giggling while the game went on around them.

"Is that the cutest thing you ever saw?" Montana C. asked me.

"It kind of is," I admitted.

When Elizabeth and Buckey got up and started running in zigzags, holding hands, Montana C. yelled to her mom, the coach, to take a video from her phone.

"We were never that little," Montana C. said to me.

"Never," I agreed.

"Come on, let's set up their doughnuts for them. Their first post-soccer doughnuts! How awesome is this?"

"Pretty awesome," I had to say.

Later there was a cookout at the town pool. A lot of the fourth-graders were hanging out at the playground. We decided to play Tag. It was fun, even though the girls were playing too and Cash hates girls, so we are all trying to also hate the girls but we're not too skilled at that.

Well, Gianni might hate them for real.

Noah likes girls and admits it.

To show the girls who's boss, we did boys-against-girls Freeze Tag. After all the boys were frozen, pretty much, we decided Freeze Tag was kind of boring so we flopped down onto the grass.

"Flop Tag," Montana C. said.

"Who's it?" Cash asked.

"Nobody!" Montana C. said.

We all just lay there in the grass for a while, like the end of a big bloody battle.

We aren't usually so quiet and still, but I guess we were all worn-out from getting back to school or running so much or maybe growing or something. Or maybe it was because the sunset was turning everything a little bit gold right then, which was a nice thing to watch happen.

Then some moms called us to come eat. It was good timing. My stomach was starting to grumble.

Montana C. turned to look at me, like, *What?*

My stomach said, *Blurble blurble bloop* again, even louder.

Montana C. laughed.

It didn't hurt my feelings, having Montana C. laugh at me and my loud belly. The opposite. That's the kind of laughter Montana C. has, which is why she is the most popular girl in third grade even though she knew transition words, which gave us extra homework.

Not third grade. I meant *fourth*.

I am not fully transitioned to fourth grade yet, I guess.

September 13, Monday

My used-to-be-best friend, Daisy, is secretly afraid of Friday the Thirteenth. That is one thing I am actually not at all afraid of. But maybe from now on I will have to be afraid of Monday the Thirteenth.

Because today I sat on a tack. I don't know who put it on my chair or if it just appeared there. I did not cry very much, not nearly as much as I could have, with all that pain. No matter what Xavier Schwartz thinks.

"That's enough, young man," Mr. Leonard said to Xavier, who right away stopped singing "Butt a-Tack! Butt a-Tack!"

Mr. Leonard asked if I wanted to go to the bathroom. I said no. The bathroom? In school? No way!

"Maybe you should pay the nurse a quick visit."

"Yeah," Noah agreed. "He could get tetanus!"

I mostly wanted everybody to stop looking at me and move on with the rest of the day—for instance, snack time. So I looked at my desk and tried becoming invisible. Mr. Leonard took my invisibile-ing as a *Yes, I would like to go to the nurse, please.* Daisy got chosen by Mr. Leonard to walk me there.

On the way, she asked, "Does it hurt?"

I was thinking about snack at that moment and what if we didn't get back in time to get any or what if there was a zombie attack before snacks could get passed out so we didn't get any pretzels, which is my favorite snack item. So I asked Daisy, "Does what hurt?" thinking she was taking about zombie attacks.

She pointed at the part of me that did actually still hurt a tiny bit.

I shook my head because what hurt most by then was my pride. The nurse gave me a throat lozenge, which tasted like shoes. I spit it out in the trash can on our way back to class. Mr. Leonard had saved us pretzels, at least.

At Free Play after lunch, the most popular song was "Butt a-Tack." I laughed along and sang it too, but on the inside I was the opposite of laughing and singing along. Maybe it was that horrible lozenge that gave me a stomachache or maybe I was getting tetanus from the tack. Or maybe rabies. Those are two of Noah's favorite diseases. It felt in my belly like probably I was getting one of those.

—— ⁓⁓⁓ ——

September 14, Tuesday

Things there should not be tests in:
Anything.
Things there especially should no way, never be tests in:
Recorder.
But tough tomatoes on me, apparently.

—— ⁓⁓⁓ ——

September 15, Wednesday

If they are going to give us a test on recorders, they should really give us more time than just two weeks. And maybe a soundproof room to practice in, so if we have a little sister, she won't go running around the whole house with her hands over her ears, screaming.

And if we have a big drooly dog, he won't act like somebody set him on fire when we just for goodness sake try to practice that horrible screechy thing.

―――

September 16, Thursday

Mr. Leonard said to choose buddies for the Make a Colonial Times Diorama or Poster—Your Choice Project.

Cash sits next to me. He turned to me right away and asked, "Buddies?" Of course, I said *yeah* to him about that.

At lunch Noah asked me whether we should do a diorama or a poster for the Colonial Times Project.

Which is why I had to say, "Oh, I already said I'd work with Cash."

"You did?" he asked. "Cash?"

"Yeah."

"The new kid?"

I nodded.

"Really?" Noah looked like he might cry.

"I just . . . I thought . . ."

26

I waited for him to finish, but he didn't. He looked very sad, so I said, "Sorry."

He walked away with his head down like he was looking for some poop to not step in.

September 17, Friday

Noah punched me in the belly while I walking back in from recess.

He said he was just swinging his arm.

But he didn't say sorry.

September 18, Saturday

Mom and Dad's anniversary is tomorrow, so they went out to dinner tonight to celebrate. Gingy and Poopsie are babysitting. They are excellent babysitters. They don't believe in bedtimes or limits on screen time. They let us have ice cream and also gummy bears and also cookies for dessert.

They probably made a bad judgment about that.

When I eat so much junk food, I get very sparky inside me.

They finally decided it was time for me to go to bed. So now I am stuck here, wide awake in my bed, while my stuffties Wingnut and Really Giraffe, who have been best friends for a long time, fight. Really Giraffe is mad because Wingnut was hanging around with Snakey at the foot of the bed, where the rough stuffties play. Wingnut tried to explain that he was just thrown there, but Really Giraffe twisted his long neck and turned away.

Wingnut felt terrible. Even when I placed him gently on the Pillow of Honor, he looked glum.

I tried talking with Really Giraffe about placement on the bed being random sometimes when I am in a rush in the morning, but he wouldn't listen. Some of the other stuffties are taking sides. Even Bananas, who is President of the Bed and usually stays out of disagreements, is annoyed with Wingnut now.

This bed is a very unfriendly place right now, full of grumbling and grudges. It is almost eleven P.M. and Mom and Dad are still not home. I think enough celebrating their anniversary is enough.

―――

September 19, Sunday

I talked with Mom about Noah and his swinging punching arm. She asked if I wanted her to talk with Noah's mom about it.

"No," I said. "Please don't."

"Well, Noah's mom and I are friends," Mom said. "I know she feels very strongly about no violence and anti-bullying rules."

"This wasn't violence or bullying," I explained. "Noah said he was just swinging his arm and my stomach was in the wrong place at the wrong time."

Mom scrunched up her face like a combination of *I doubt it* and *Wow, that was a sour lemon I just ate.*

That made me smile. I like when Mom is funny and on my side.

She said a bunch of stuff about how Noah should use his words instead of his fists. And also, best of all, that she was very proud of me for saying, "Please stop," instead of just hitting Noah back, because violence doesn't solve anything.

<u>However</u>: I might have made up the part where I said, *Please stop,* instead of just *Oof.*

Still, though, maybe Mom is right to be proud of me. Other than that little lie I told. I mean, exaggeration. But maybe I am pretty good at friendship and behavior, because of not hitting Noah back in *his* belly. I didn't think of doing that, is the truth. But maybe it's not because I am a scared kid or a not-think-of-the-idea-of-punching-back kid. Maybe I am a good kid. Maybe I am good at being nonviolent, and at being a friend.

A lot better than I am at the recorder, anyway. Well, Gingy and Poopsie love how I play the recorder. They could listen to me play the recorder all day long.

It probably helps that they don't hear very well, but I appreciated the praise anyway.

September 20, Monday

Luckily, I don't have to take violin after school anymore because I was terrible and also my teacher moved to Nebraska. I don't think she moved just to get away from me, but I am not sure.

SKREE·ONK!!

Instead of violin lessons, I have more free time, so today I went over to Cash's house after school to work on our Colonial America project. He walks home. No school bus, no grown-up picking him up. He just points himself toward home and then walks there. I don't think my mom knew that, but it was too late.

Cash has two older sisters, it turns out. They are in eighth grade, and they look exactly alike because they are identical twins. So they are exactly as pretty as each other.

Which is very.

They were in the kitchen when we got to Cash's house and they both said hi, but the way they say it, it's more like *haaaaaaa*, like a long happy sigh. I don't know what their names are because of their accents from Tennessee. Both names sounded like just a lot of vowels. But with a giggle hidden inside and also maybe some singing. So I didn't call either of them any name.

I said, "Oh, okay. I am Justin."

Which they thought was *adorable*! I don't know why exactly.

I meant to say they had a beautiful home, but I wasn't sure if you just say that to grown-ups, so then I just said hi again. But in the regular way, not like *haaaaaaa*.

They made us a snack of ice cream in bowls. The reason I got ice cream all over one of my cheeks was because I forgot where my mouth was, with those extremely pretty teenagers giggling and saying stuff like *adorable*! One of them said that I *was just the cutest thing ever!* and would I be her boyfriend? Then the other one said, *No, I saw him first!*

I didn't say much of anything.

After our snack, Cash and I went to his room and played with all his stuff at once. No grown-ups came to say Not So Wild in the House. Because no grown-ups were in the house. Just two teenage girls and us.

We didn't get one single thing done on our Colonial America project and there was my dad, picking me up. Cash said, "So what? We'll throw something together eventually."

I said, of course, *yeah*.

In my family kids are not allowed to stay in the house without grown-ups. We are not even allowed to say *So what*.

Cash is the luckiest guy on the planet.

―⁓⁓―

September 21, Tuesday

There was a surprise math test today.

Division.

I love division.

I love fourth grade.

I love coming in from lunch and seeing *100%* on the top of my paper.

Sometimes life is so excellent.

―⁓⁓―

September 22, Wednesday

At recess there was a choice of stay in to work on recorder with Ms. Zhang or go outside to play. Ms. Zhang recommended stay in for extra help for anybody who was having trouble with hitting the right notes or getting a nice flowing sound.

Noah picked up his recorder in its velvet bag and my

recorder in its velvet bag. With one in each hand, like he was going to twirl batons, Noah yelled, "Come on, Justin!"

Cash, at that same exact second, was also saying, "Come on, Justin Case!" But he was going in the opposite direction, toward the playground.

I stood there in between them, looking one way and then looking the other way.

"Justin!" Noah waved the two velvet bags at me. "You know you need extra help! Let's go!"

I said, "No, I'm good."

That was a lie. I am not good. My recorder-playing breath isn't a smooth steady breeze like Ms. Zhang wants it to be. It's more of a gasping. Or a burping.

PHWEET

I know that. I know I need extra help.
I know the test is coming up next week. But
I also really needed to just play outside for
a little while.

And I guess I was a little mad that Noah yelled out to everybody that I needed extra help. He didn't have to do that. So I went on with the kids who were going outside to play.

Now that I am in my room, setting up my Knights for an epic battle, I am starting to wonder if maybe I made a very dumb choice.

Wingnut thinks I should just practice extra tonight to make up for it.

Really Giraffe thinks Wingnut should butt out.

Snakey thinks if I make those horrible noises on my recorder again, somebody might bite me in my sleep. Even though his teeth are soft and stuffed, they could be magically venomous.

And the Knights, who are also big Not Fans of "Hot Cross Buns," have weapons.

―――

September 23, Thursday

Noah had three Oreos in his lunch box. Three Oreos is one serving, he said; it's on the box. That is why he couldn't share even half of one Oreo with me. Because then he wouldn't have his full serving.

I had only carrots as my to-go-with-the-sandwich part of my lunch. Noah knows this sometimes happens to me. Usually he is very generous during the hard times of my mom's Health Kicks, when I have dried-out carrot planks in a Baggie next to my lunch box and a frown on my face.

"Don't your parents own a candy store?" Cash asked.

"Yeah," I answered.

"So they should be all about junk food."

"Yeah," I agreed.

"You obviously don't know Justin's parents," Noah said.

"No packaged candy or cookies," I explained. "And sometimes my mom goes on a Health Kick, so there's only vegetables and wheat germ."

"Youch," Cash said. He held out his bag of potato chips to me. I took a couple. They were just the shards, and very greasy.

Not as delicious as an Oreo, but still good. Better than dried-out carrot planks.

"Maybe if I had four Oreos," Noah said, biting into his first one, "then I could help you out."

Cash held out his potato chips to me again. I shook my

head. I didn't want to take advantage of his generosity. Also maybe I wanted Noah to see I wasn't a greedy kid.

"Maybe you could sneak me one tomorrow," I asked Noah. "Or, like, just one part, the bottom half. You wouldn't even have to share the creme filling."

Bartholomew Wiggins came over and sat down at our table. "I was doing some extra recorder practice with Ms. Zhang. Why didn't you guys come? It was very helpful," he said. "Hey, Oreos! Can I have one?"

Without looking up at me, Noah gave Bartholomew Wiggins a whole Oreo, creme filling and all. Which made me think maybe the problem was not just about the size of a complete serving.

But when I mentioned that, Noah answered that he and Bartholomew Wiggins had to discuss their Colonial Times Diorama so please stop interrupting them about my food issues.

—~~~—

September 24, Friday

Today in music class we sounded like a traffic jam.

Ms. Zhang smiled a lot, but maybe that is the kind of smile called wincing.

September 25, Saturday

Cash came over to work on the Colonial Times Project while Dad and Elizabeth were at Elizabeth's soccer game and Mom was trying to read the paper in peace for a few minutes, please. So we just ran around outside with Qwerty instead of figuring out a Colonial Times Project to be working on.

"We'll get it done, Justin," Cash said. "Don't worry about it."

I am trying that, but Not Worrying is not my best skill.

September 26, Sunday

Tomorrow is our recorder test. All my stuffties and knights are very relieved we will be done with that thing finally. Really Giraffe thinks chess would be a better thing for them to teach in music class. I tried to explain that chess is not a musical instrument, but Really Giraffe ignored me. Maybe because giraffes have no vocal cords.

I don't know if that is actually true, but it is what Noah said one time.

Today at the soccer game, after scoring his second goal, Cash said he is going to be a professional soccer player when he grows up. Noah said Silly Putty is actually a liquid.

I only believe one of them.

Hint: It is not the one who probably made that thing up about giraffes too.

—◆—

September 27, Monday

The bad news:

The Recorder Test was today.

The good news:

We all had to play "Hot Cross Buns" together, not one at a time.

The even better news:

I didn't fail.

The reason I didn't fail:

Cash whispered to me right before we started, "Just kazoo it."

What that meant:

"Pretend you're playing but don't really blow into it,"

Cash explained. "Just hum the tune and move your fingers around."

What I did:

kazooed it.

My humming was the very quiet kind of humming, not the *who-who-who* humming I do on my actual kazoo. Our class did not sound great, but if you knew what tune we were supposed to be playing, you could sort of, a little, hear bits of it wandering around inside the goose-ish honking noise.

"Wonderful," Ms. Zhang said afterward, and clapped. Xavier Schwartz bowed. I just stood there holding on to my recorder while my belly kazooed its own new, original song.

The title of the song my belly was playing:

"Yeah, But That Kind of Not-Failing Is Also Maybe Called Cheating."

September 28, Tuesday

Today Cash and I didn't do our Colonial Times project.

Again.

I tried to discuss the situation with Mom and Dad at dinner, about what should you do if you are partners with somebody on a project and the partner keeps saying *Don't worry, we'll get it done* every time you say *Maybe we should work on our project.*

But before I could ask the full question, Elizabeth interrupted to say, *Oh, speaking of projects, do we have Poster Board because I have to make a project on the rain cycle and it's due tomorrow.*

We didn't clear our plates. Not even Mom. She and Dad were both too busy looking at their watches and grumbling and tilting their heads at each other to deal with dishes. We had to get in the car right away to go dashing all over town to find an open store to buy Poster Board.

A new rule in our family is *You Are Not Allowed to Say "Poster Board" after six* P.M.

My shiny white . . . thing that I am not allowed to say because it is night . . . and my new pack of markers they also got me (just me, the full eight-pack, no sharing) as a bonus are all ready for my Colonial Times project.

Just in case Cash and I ever actually do our Colonial Times project.

But he wasn't over and we are supposed to work as a team, so I put my supplies upstairs in my room and went down to watch Mom and Dad help Elizabeth glue cotton balls to a big blue Poster Board for her project on clouds. Her clouds are cumulus, which is the opposite of rain clouds. Elizabeth kept getting distracted from making her poster because all she wanted to do was explain the rain cycle to us.

"We know about the rain cycle," Dad said. "It's bedtime, sweetheart. Let's try to get this done."

Elizabeth stood up and stomped on the glue bottle.

"Elizabeth!" Mom yelled.

"Oh, yeah?" Elizabeth shouted. "Do you know the song that goes 'Precipitation, evaporation, condensation, begin again'?"

"Yes," we all said.

I had the same first-grade teacher she has. Of course I know "Precipitation, evaporation, condensation, begin again." It was my favorite song in first grade.

She stomped up to her room to have a tantrum so Mom and Dad had to chase her while I went to my room to try not to listen to that whole disaster of cumulus clouds and glue and tantrums and then a dog who had his own ideas about a good project to do with glue and paint and cotton balls.

—*mm*—

September 29, Wednesday

In Colonial Times, people rode horses, wore weird clothes, including shoes with buckles on them, and hated a fat king who lived in England and wanted to tax them with stamps.

So next week we are going on a class trip.

—*mm*—

September 30, Thursday

Cash came over after school to work on our project again. Luckily, it was raining out so we couldn't spend the afternoon in the backyard with Qwerty. After some sword fights and snacks, we got down to business. Mom asked if we needed some help, but Cash said, "No, thank you, ma'am."

Mom blinked a couple of times at that. "Oh, um, okeydoke," she said, and then, after a very shattering crash from the kitchen, she yelled, "Elizabeth! Stay very still and touch nothing!"

Cash sat in the chair in front of the computer and clicked around. I stood beside him, watching. "How about this?" he asked me.

He had found a game that kids played in Colonial Times. It was called Nine Men's Morris and it seemed kind of complicated but kind of simple. Simple enough for us to make on the poster board, but a little complicated to play. In a good way.

"It's perfect!" Cash said. "Plus we'll get to play it."

"Yeah," I agreed.

"Got a ruler?" he asked.

An hour later we had the game all made. We decided to use beans for me and marshmallows for him, but then we ate the marshmallows. So we used some rocks from Elizabeth's rock collection (*In Our Family We Share*). We played until Cash's dad came to pick him up.

It is the best project I ever made for school.

After dinner I taught Mom, Dad, and Elizabeth how to play Nine Men's Morris. They all liked it. Mom liked it way better than chess. Dad said Cash and I could make millions on it. Elizabeth said it was the best game ever.

I was pretty famous in my family for a while tonight. It was very cool.

We played the whole time until bedtime without even stopping to watch TV or have dessert. That's how good this game is.

I wonder if Noah made something cool too, and if he's still mad at me.

If he is, he could join forces with Elizabeth, who recognized her rocks after the third time she played.

I had to make new ones out of Play-Doh, which didn't exist in Colonial Times, but poopie diapers on me because it was bedtime. Hopefully Cash won't be mad about that tomorrow.

Now I can't sleep because I keep thinking, *Yeah, but he might be.*

Things I am good at getting:

    1. Friends mad at me.

—ᴍᴍ—

October 1, Friday

"They're great," Cash said when I showed him the Play-Doh rock substitutes. "They look good. No worries."

Each team had two minutes to present their project. Mr. Leonard made a frowny face when Cash and I showed ours. But it wasn't a sad type of frown. More like an impressed frown.

We all spend a lot of time discussing what Mr. Leonard's expressions mean. The fifth-graders told us at lunch yesterday that it takes at least until March, but we can't wait that long.

Noah and Bartholomew Wiggins made a diorama. Mr. Leonard tipped his head a little to the side. Nobody knows what that means.

I wasn't sure what the diorama showed. I think it was something to do with Colonial People making spices and how that did something to help win the Revolution. But I'm not

sure. A cool thing was that you could open the baggies and smell the spices.

Mr. Leonard says it's important to come up with something positive to say about other people's work. It's called a feedback sandwich—something positive, something they could improve, and then for the other piece of bread, something else positive. Fourth grade is very complicated with rules of everything, including how to talk to one another.

There was a big crowd around Nine Men's Morris at recess. I decided to take a break from playing so other kids could get a turn. I wandered over to Noah and said, for the bottom piece of bread in my feedback sandwich, "I like how you can smell the spices in the baggies."

Noah didn't hear me.

So I tried again. I said, "Hey, Noah, it's cool, that smelly element of your project."

Noah said, "Shut up."

Which you are not allowed to say in my family or in school or probably even in Noah's family, where there are very few rules.

October 2, Saturday

My favorite thing about soccer is after the game, you get to eat doughnuts.

My second favorite thing is sometimes it rains and you don't have to play.

Unfortunately, today was sunny and warm. The only cloud was a cumulus, like on Elizabeth's poster before Qwerty wrecked it. So, no rain would come no matter how much soccer kids might wish for it. Not from a cumulus that was floating all lazy and perfect right over the soccer field. It looked more like a bunch of cotton balls stuck together than the stuck-together cotton balls had. Dopey cumulus. I was just looking at it for one second.

Unfortunately, that was the one second when Cash kicked the ball hard toward my cheek.

I wasn't crying. It was just eye wetness that the ball knocked loose, is all. Cash doesn't know everything. He and Sam Pasternak think they are so great just because their feet get along well with soccer balls.

It was hard to even chew a soft doughnut after the game with my face still throbbing so much. But I toughed it out and ate two. Because I *am* tough. Even tough kids have eye wetness. That's what keeps our eyeballs from popping out of our head like gum balls from a machine.

—mm—

October 3, Sunday

My whole family got invited to Montana C.'s house for brunch before Elizabeth and Buckey's soccer game. Elizabeth wore a ninja costume. When Mom suggested maybe she should wear something more brunch appropriate, Elizabeth

 explained that a ninja costume was appropriate because someday she might marry Buckey.

Mom tried to argue with Elizabeth about that not making any sense as a reason to wear a ninja costume to brunch, but Mom's weapon was Logic. Elizabeth's weapon was Ninja Magic Superpower.

 Logic is a pretty weak weapon sometimes, it turns out.

I should get some Ninja Magic Superpower.

I tried to use the lesser-superpowers of Whining and Complaining and Explaining. No luck. I wanted to get

left home alone to relax for goodness sake but my not-so-superpowers did not do the trick. If Cash is old enough to stay home alone, I am too. I had a long hard week of being with people, especially girls, which I *no thank you*, plus the cheek injury. And then brunch too? How much can one guy take?

Mom countered with "Justin! In the car NOW."

There is no non-ninja defense against that.

But here is the secret nobody can know: I had fun with Montana C. even though she is a girl, and even though she beat me at air hockey four out of the five times we played while we stayed at her house instead of going to the little kid soccer game.

―――

October 4, Monday

Our desks got shuffled into groups and Montana C.'s ended up right next to mine.

"Our next project will be for science," Mr. Leonard said. "You're going to map the floor of an imaginary ocean."

Then he kept talking. I don't know what he said. I wasn't listening because I had a lot of thoughts crashing around inside my head, like:

How do you map the floor of an ocean that isn't even real?

How do you *map*? Is that a thing? *Map* can be a verb?

Does it just mean Make a Map? Or is it a synonym for *mop*?

And why didn't anybody tell me before this that there is a floor in the ocean? It must be under a lot of sand because when I went in it this summer at Gingy and Poopsie's beach condo, I sure didn't feel any tiles or rugs or other floor things down there.

I managed to not smile, imagining mopping the floor of the ocean, mopping up all the wet until there was just floor, and where would I dump the bucket of mopped-up ocean water?

And right then, which I know because I was just wondering if Montana C.'s brother Buckey's real name is Bucket, Montana C. leaned over and wrote on a page in the science section of my notebook:

Partners?

So I wrote back, under that:

OK.

Then she drew a smiley face.

I drew hair on it.

Then I felt Mr. Leonard looking at me, so I stopped that behavior before I could ask the question of *Is your brother's real name Bucket?* But I still didn't pay any attention to Mr. Leonard's words. I think I might have been hypnotized into a trance or something because all I did was stare at the page of my notebook that had Montana C.'s ink on it.

Nobody other than me or a teacher ever wrote in my notebook before, is maybe why I was all tranced-up.

When I lifted my head, everybody was gathering their stuff to go home. Noah stood, hovering over my desk.

"So?" he asked.

"What?" I asked, making *so what,* but it doesn't count when it happens like that, I am pretty sure.

"So do you want to be partners on the science project? Or are you working with Cash again?"

I swallowed hard. "Oh. No."

"Cool, because I was thinking we could—"

"Um," I interrupted. "Montana C."

Noah stared at me. "What about her?"

"Is," I said. "My."

"Montana C. is your *what?*" Noah asked, way too loudly.

"Is the, I'm working," I whispered. "I said I'd be partners with her."

"When?" he yelled. "When did you even have a chance to— Justin, I don't believe . . ."

"Sorry, Noah. I . . ."

He kicked the leg of my chair and stormed away.

October 5, Tuesday

In gym we started a unit of Tug-of-War. There is no worse game than that.

Even if you win, you end up on your butt with skinned palms.

If you lose, you're in a pile of losers with your nose smooshed onto the back of other really annoyed kids.

Plus why would they want us to play stuff with "War" in it? Why can't we just have Run Around Having Fun as our sport?

⸺

October 6, Wednesday

I went to Noah's house for a playdate. Like always, we had cookies and milk at his kitchen counter with his mom, who asked how was our day. After we finished, we went up to Noah's room for one round of Battleship and then played on Noah's computer. He has his own and he gets unlimited screen time. He says it is not a proven scientific fact that too much screen time makes your brain rot. It is an old wives' tale. Which means not true.

After about an hour, our eyes were all googly, but our brains were supposedly not rotting and no old wives had said to stop.

It was like old times.

But then Noah asked if I wanted another snack, and I said sure because who doesn't want another snack? So we went down to the kitchen to choose something, and he took out a big box of Rice Krispies Treats.

"Awesome," I said.

"Oh, no," he said. "I forgot. We can't have these because I am saving them for some friends I have coming over tomorrow. We can have a plum."

He wouldn't say which friends are coming over tomorrow. He made it sound like there was going to be a party. I don't know why I was invited for the day before the party instead of for the party when there were going to be Rice Krispies Treats, which I actually really enjoy and Noah knows that.

He knows that because we have been second-best friends for a very long time.

When Dad picked me up, after the playdate, I was in a grumpy mood. I did not feel like talking about it. Anyway, it's not the kind of thing Noah would get put in trouble for, giving me a plum for second snack. Even if he sort of should.

I wish he would be put in trouble for a big long time, in fact.

But he won't. His mom calls him "angel face" and gives him anything he wants, like Rice Krispies Treats and unlimited screen time and parties when it isn't even his birthday. So he isn't likely to be put in trouble over what he did.

Or ever.

All I have to do is forget to make my bed and into trouble I go.

—

October 7, Thursday

Our field trip to a Colonial Farm is tomorrow. We have to bring our recorders because we will be playing them there as if we were Colonial children. We are playing a Colonial tune called "Fife and Drum." I hope somebody learned some of the notes, because I am definitely going to have to kazoo it again.

If we all kazoo, we will just be a bunch of non-Colonial children holding recorders while humming. We will get in so much trouble if that happens.

Cash said, "Don't worry. The girls have been practicing."

Xavier Schwartz said, "Justin Case is the king of worrying."

"He can't help it," Gianni Schicci added.

I concentrated on making the cardboard-and-tinfoil buckle I have to tape onto my sneakers for tomorrow instead of arguing about if I can or can't help worrying. Within the minute, they were talking about the fact that Rozzie Constantine was absent because she has pinkeye and whether pinkeye is caused by somebody farting on your eye or not. Rozzie Constantine has,

like, ten younger brothers who never stop running around except to be gross, so the chances of one of them farting on her eye is high.

So now I wonder if that is actually the cause of pinkeye. I almost asked Noah, who would know if that is truly how you get it.

But I don't feel like it, honestly. I know he used his words instead of his fists at our playdate, but my belly still hurt all night afterward.

―――

October 8, Friday

I have to ask Poopsie if he was a kid during Colonial Times. Colonial kids had chores all day long, and no screen time at all. They must've been so mad.

On the other hand, we got to hammer a nail into a ring shape and keep it, smell disgusting spices, shake cream until it turned into butter, and watch a donkey pooping.

Class trips are The Bomb.

The Bomb means excellent in Cash's language.

Mr. Leonard is also The Bomb, because he let us play Tag on the field instead of doing a second round of performing on our recorders. Ms. Zhang looked disappointed, but the tour guides looked very delighted.

—⁓—

October 9, Saturday

I spent all morning working on Halloween costume ideas. Elizabeth said she wanted to go either as a Ninja or as our dog, Qwerty. She already goes to school most of the time this year as a Ninja, though, so nobody would even realize she was in a costume if she went as a Ninja. They would just think, *Oh, there's Elizabeth.*

She said, "Well, I could add blood."

Mom said no. Even when we explained that it could be fake blood.

So we worked on making Elizabeth a Qwerty costume.

It took a lot of glue and toilet paper, but it looked so good, I was thinking I might want to go as Qwerty too.

Woof! —

By then it was raining really hard and Mom was watching the news, which said there might be a hurricane. So all the soccer games were canceled and we got to spent the afternoon trying to de-toilet-paper Elizabeth and clean up this mess because what in the world were we thinking.

—*nnn*—

October 10, Sunday

It rained and rained all night and then all day. The wind slammed against our house so hard, Qwerty hid under me every place I sat. Elizabeth tried to explain the rain cycle to all of us again. We still knew it. Even Qwerty didn't want to hear about precipitation, condensation, and evaporation again.

When enough was enough with the Rain Cycle song, Mom turned on the TV. A movie in the middle of the day. "Yay! Yay yay yay!" Elizabeth and I cheered. We had a little celebration parade around the living room before we sunk down on the couch to watch *The Wizard of Oz*.

Mom wasn't watching that much because she kept checking weather news on her computer the whole time. And Dad was in the bedroom watching the football game.

But then the electricity went out.

We looked for flashlights for a while. Then we sat in the dark, listening to the wind screaming and also Dad yelling that he DID put the flashlights away last time and somebody else must have taken them.

Elizabeth and I decided to look upstairs because maybe we did take them. We couldn't remember. We stuck together, because of the dark and the screaming wind and the yelling parents and especially because of the movie. Maybe *The Wizard of Oz* wasn't such a great choice during a storm.

Elizabeth kept feeling the house starting to lift up into the air.

She also was absolutely sure she heard witch-on-a-bicycle music outside.

"It wasn't," I told her. "That wasn't witch-bike music. Definitely not."

I am pretty confident I was telling the truth. I might have heard it a little bit too, but maybe one of our neighbors was also watching that movie somehow despite the blackout. Or bike riding.

Or we were both just remembering the music or hearing an echo of it in our minds or something.

Probably that's it. Though Mrs. Worthington in the dark house at the top of the Dead End does look a little witchy.

We went back downstairs with zero flashlights. Mom lit some candles.

We blew them out after one minute because Qwerty was in a rush to get everywhere at once. Elizabeth too. "Qwerty will not fit into the basket of my bike!" Elizabeth screamed.

"Everybody calm the heck down!" Mom yelled. "Right this minute!"

Elizabeth flew into Mom's arms and knocked her onto the chair. Mom sighed and wrapped her arms around Elizabeth, who curled up tight there.

Mom smiled at me like I was so calm and brave, and like she felt proud of that. What I did not tell her was that I was just slower at figuring out where to go. Otherwise I might have been the one curled up in that lap of hers.

I just sat all alone on the couch in my own tight little scrunch.

"Okay," Dad said. Sometimes he just says okay without knowing what is going on at all. "Okay."

Even though it was dangerous, Dad decided he and I should put on our rain gear and head over to our store to put wood in the windows so they wouldn't shatter.

I am not a big fan of doing stuff that comes in a sentence after the words *even though it's dangerous.*

We had to use the windshield wipers on their fastest so they sounded like *flink flunk flink flunk flink flunck!* Dad didn't even turn on the radio or sing.

After we got all the planks of wood in place in the front windows and made *X*s with masking tape on the other windows, he put his hands on his hips and smiled at me. "Well," he said. "Best we can do."

He took down the jar of chocolate-covered graham crackers. Mom had made a fresh batch yesterday. Chocolate-covered graham crackers are our store's top sellers after malt balls.

A newspaper review of our store that was in the paper three years ago mentioned the chocolate-covered graham crackers especially. There was a picture of the chocolate-covered graham crackers with *Worth the trip!* in a blotch of red next to them. There was also a picture of the four of us in front of the store, Elizabeth in Dad's arms because she was so little and wouldn't stop running all over the place while the photographer was trying to snap a picture. That was cool. I was famous for being in the paper after that for about a week or maybe two, in first grade.

Wow, I was Elizabeth's now-age, then. I thought I was so old.

Chocolate-covered graham crackers are my favorite food after gummy worms. Sometimes I get one for a special treat. Today Dad gave me FOUR for being so helpful and brave.

I ate two—one in the store and one in the car. They were excellent. I gave one of them to Elizabeth when we got home because she is only a first-grader lap-sitter. It's not her fault that she didn't get asked to go to the store to help.

By then the lights had come back on, so she was watching a second whole movie, a cartoon one with no weather in it, but still, it was, like, a total of about a hundred hours of screen time for her. But I gave her one of my chocolate covered-graham crackers anyway, because I wanted to be a good big brother.

Also I knew that was the kind of thing that would make Mom and Dad really proud, sharing when you aren't forced to. They love stuff like that. And I was getting a little addicted to hearing what a good boy I was. I admit it.

I saved the fourth one to give to Noah, because chocolate-covered graham crackers by my mom are his favorites too.

But even though Mom and Dad both said again what a great kid I am when they kissed me good night, I might not end up giving that chocolate-covered graham cracker to Noah. All my stuffties are having a meeting about if I am mean or doing the right thing if I keep it for myself.

It does not feel excellent to be leaning toward doing what Snakey thinks I should do instead of what Wingnut and Bananas think is right.

I might get up and eat that thing myself anyway. Even though I already brushed my teeth and it's very late. That's how rough I am feeling. Rough as the hurricane that blew itself out and knocked down so many trees.

Rough enough to eat my second-best friend (or is he?)'s chocolate-covered graham cracker RIGHT NOW.

October 11, Monday

Mr. Leonard says a good way to jump-start our creative writing is to make lists. I thought it was transition words. But I guess not anymore. Today we had to do a list of our top three worries and then share them with the writing groups we got put into.

My Top 3 Worries by Justin K.:

1. Getting eaten by a bullhead shark

2. Falling off a cliff

3. Brain rot from too much screen time

Noah's Top 3 Worries:

1. Hurricanes that knock a tree onto his mom's car

2. Diseases

3. Robbers

Cash's Top 3 Worries:

1. Sleepaway camp

2. Sleepaway college

3. That Mr. Leonard is secretly an Evil Spy Warlord or possibly an Alien

---

October 12, Tuesday

My New Top 3 Worries:

Same as Cash's, except for the one about Mr. Leonard.

I never thought of worrying about sleepaway camp or sleepaway college before today. But now I am making up for lost time on those worries. Also a little bit about trees falling on our car. And diseases. Plus Xavier Schwartz's big brother.

Okay, maybe also a little that Mr. Leonard is an Evil Spy Warlord or Alien.

This might not have been exactly the type of jump-starting my life needed.

—————

October 13, Wednesday

Mom said "Don't be so silly, Justin—Mr. Leonard is just a teacher." He is a very quiet, smart, and strict teacher, it's true. And very tall, and a man, but still, he is just a teacher. He doesn't have mind control OR mind-reading powers.

I really don't think he has any of those. I was just wondering what they thought. Dad thinks maybe Mr. Leonard is an alien.

I am 92 percent sure Dad was joking about that, and I do not get what he meant about I should bring Reese's Pieces to school and see what happens, but I am happy to bring candy no matter what reason. You get big crowds around you for stuff like that, and in a very good way. But then he didn't give me candy to bring.

Probably Cash is just kidding about the alien stuff too. He probably just wants to see which kids are goofy enough to fall for it. Xavier might be that goofy. Or else he just can't help agreeing with Cash about everything. Like the rest of us.

Me and Cash and Xavier weren't scared of the hurricane. Mr. Leonard's mind-control tricks (if he really does have mind-control tricks, which he doesn't) couldn't make us think we were, at least so far.

A lot of girls and also Noah were still talking today about how scared they were during the hurricane. Cash said Mr. Leonard was mind-controlling them to think they were scared even if they weren't.

I'm not so sure. Noah has been scared of weather his whole life.

October 14, Thursday

For homework last night, we had to write a personal essay about our experiences in the hurricane and then share it with the group today. I was in Group B.

Not because I am in the middle level of smartness. It's not like with reading groups or math groups. It's random.

We had to give constructive criticism on each other's essays.

I spent a lot of time last night making lists of something personal that I was willing to have kids in my class read and criticize. Constructive or not, it's still *criticism*. I used up a lot of pieces of paper and chewed the eraser off my pencil.

The one I chose from my list was about how scared my dog was. I know that is not about me personally, but I was out of time. Plus the eraser crumbles were very challenging to get off my tongue. So that was that.

All night I dreamed that Mr. Leonard and Qwerty were chasing me down hallways, and both of them were trying to bite me. It was not a restful night, which is why I looked like a zombie at school today.

A lot of the runny-aroundy boys are in Group B. They thought my personal essay was very funny. They kept saying to the girls in Group B, "Justin Case's DOG was scared of the hurricane." And then they were trying out howling like Qwerty until Mr. Leonard raised his right eyebrow. That thing is like a MUTE button.

After Mr. Leonard walked away, Xavier Schwartz whispered to Cash, "Was Mr. Leonard mind-controlling Qwerty?"

"He probably was," Cash whispered back.

"Yeah," Xavier said.

Group B's constructive criticism of my essay was:

> Qwerty is The Bomb.

Also that getting eaten by a bullhead shark is way scarier than a hurricane or if your teacher actually is an Evil Spy Warlord Alien.

Cash said, "You say that *now*."

That shut us all up as completely as Mr. Leonard's eyebrow.

—*mm*—

October 15, Friday

I think I got the definition right, but the spelling wrong of the word *kerfuffle*. It means "a fuss" *or* "commotion." But I am not sure how many dozens of *fff*'s it has. I just know it is Mr. Leonard's favorite word, as in "Let's stop that kerfuffle now, please."

After that test, we were supposed to have Silent Reading Time. Well, all the other teachers in our whole school call it

Silent Reading Time. Mr. Leonard calls it BOOOCH, which makes it sound way cooler, so everybody in 4-L looks forward to it.

BOOOCH stands for Books of Our Own CHoice.

And our favorite thing in the day is when Mr. Leonard, whose voice is usually very quiet and calm, yells, very loud and long, "BOOOCH!" We all get to run to the bookshelves or our backpacks and pick out our BOOOCHes and then flop anywhere we feel like flopping for a few excellent quiet reading moments. Even the kids who never liked reading before get very happy when Mr. Leonard bellows *BOOOCH!*

But today during BOOOCH, we got a choice of flopping with our BOOOCH books or using the time to work on our maps of the imaginary ocean floor.

That was a good thing because I had forgotten all about the map of the imaginary ocean floor. And the final project is due on Monday. I love BOOOCH, but Montana C. and I went with mapping.

We stared together at a blank piece of loose-leaf in Montana C.'s notebook. I wasn't thinking about imaginary oceans, though. I was thinking, *I wish Mr. Leonard would make up his mind about what we are supposed to be concentrating on.* He says, "The key to success is Focus." But as soon as I get focused on vocab or spelling things right or making lists or criticizing constructively, all of a sudden we're supposed to be doing other stuff I don't know how to do like long-dividing by three-digit numbers or playing recorder or Tug-of-War.

Or making maps of imaginary places with girls who say stuff like, "You should come over this weekend and we can work on our map—and have an air hockey rematch."

And then dealing with boys who are all saying stuff like, "Ooooo!"

―――

October 16, Saturday

A thing I love:

Winning soccer games.

A thing I *no, thank you*:

My dad, who is the coach, picking up a boy named Cash instead of a boy named Justin—and calling the lifted boy Champ and Atta Boy, which are what he should call me even if that other kid is better at kicking a soccer ball.

Also riding a scooter. Cash and Xavier Schwartz and Gianni Schicci and Sam Pasternak and Montana C. all ride scooters. Cash said I could have a turn on his, but I almost fell over in one second of trying.

Maybe if I had my own scooter, I could practice in private before I try it out in front of people. But Mom said, "We'll see, buddy," about that, which means *That looks way too dangerous so no way, buddy.*

October 17, Sunday

Here is what my first draft map of the imaginary ocean floor looked like:

Here is what Montana C.'s first draft of the imaginary ocean floor looked like:

Here is what our final draft map of the imaginary ocean floor looked like:

Oil pastels are the most awesome crayons ever. In my family you have to put down newspaper because they make such a mess and then after five minutes Mom says, *Okay, let's put these horrible things I never should have bought away in the high-up cabinet and try to get the stains off the table now.*

It is not our fault newspaper sometimes slides.

But at Montana C.'s house there is a worktable in the basement, and all the pastels you want anytime you want to use them right out there where kids can reach them, in a can, and you don't even have to clean up the stains afterward. And there weren't even any first-graders there because they had their soccer game to go to.

Our map is the kind that has bumpy bits. We made them out of rubber cement and two pieces of used bubble gum. We each chewed one and then stuck it to the map.

Luckily, I am a good gum-chewer, so I did add something constructive to the project.

If we don't get the best grade Mr. Leonard ever gave for a map of an imaginary ocean floor, we will both die of shock because, seriously, this is the best thing EVER. Better than if you could do wheelies on your scooter. Better than gummy worms, maybe.

The chewed-up gum part is a secret just between me and Montana C. We will never tell anybody ever.

―――

October 18, Monday

Noah worked alone on his project. His project was:

A blank blue poster board with a big papier-mâché fish taped on top.

It took me some time, but I thought of a positive statement to start my constructive criticism of that off with. As we were arranging our projects on the tables, I whispered to Noah, "That's a really cool-looking fish, Noah."

Noah smiled really big. "Thanks, Justin. I worked on it all weekend. It's a Sloane's viperfish. Is that your project?"

I nodded.

"It's very . . . bumpy."

"Yeah." I am not sure if bumpy counts as a positive.

"What's it made of?"

"Never mind that!" I leaned close to Noah's ear so nobody would hear. I didn't want him to get in trouble. "There's still time," I whispered. "You could quickly just draw on the poster board."

"Draw what?" Noah asked.

"A *map!*" I yanked Noah's shirt to pull him a little away from all the other kids listening. "We were supposed to make a map of an imaginary ocean floor. That was the assignment, Noah. Mr. Leonard said—"

Noah interrupted in his booming voice, "The Sloane's viperfish holds the world record for largest teeth relative to head size in a fish."

"Okay," I said.

Noah crossed his arms, like he'd won.

"You're a Sloane's viperfish," Xavier Schwartz said to Noah.

"No, he's not," Cash said.

I smiled at Cash because, well, that was nice, I thought. Standing up for Noah like that. Even though Noah has never been very nice to Cash.

But then Cash said, "He's the opposite of a Sloane's viperfish because he has the hugest head of any kid I ever saw."

"And the littlest teeth," Xavier Schwartz added.

Noah just stood there blinking for a few seconds, and then he stomped away, leaving his papier-mâché Sloane's viperfish staring at us like it might bite our heads off.

October 19, Tuesday

Top ten things I am worried about, Science Project edition:

1. Standing at the front of the room next to Montana C. and speaking up.

2. What are we going to say if anybody asks, "Is there any chewed gum on there?"

3. Because I promised Montana C. that I would never tell anybody that.

4. But what if Mr. Leonard says, *Please answer the question, young man?*

5. Noah presenting his project because his is still not a map of the imaginary ocean floor: it is still just a papier-mâché of a Sloane's viperfish, despite the extra day we got.

6. Even if you are a big fan of the Sloane's viperfish, and even if Sloane's viperfish are in the book of *Guinness World Records* for their big teeth-to-head ratio, it is still not an okay project if the teacher said to make a map of an imaginary ocean floor.

7. Although Noah has been kind of mean to me lately, I still don't want him to get in trouble in school.

8. Maybe with his mom.

9. But not in school. Because he is still my friend.

10. And there are limits.

―――

October 20, Wednesday

Didn't get called on again. Phew.

Neither did Noah. Phew.

Xavier Schwartz and Cash went though. Theirs was awesome. It had moving parts and glitter. Our innovation of chewed gum seems less cool now than it used to.

And in gym we have moved on from Tug-of-War. Which is great except that Native Americans long ago played a game called lacrosse so now we have to too.

―――

October 21, Thursday

How are we supposed to keep track of the independent reading AND how to spell stuff AND what new song we're supposed to know how to play on the recorder when at any moment we could be called on to explain why there is chewed gum and what the heck is that mess in the corner where I messed up, so what, people mess up sometimes. I tried to make it look like a lake, but I am now realizing, too late, that how can there be a lake on the ocean floor? Even if it is imaginary?

There is too much going on. My head is pounding so, so hard. And I haven't even figured out Halloween yet.

—*—

October 22, Friday

First kids called to present their map of an imaginary ocean floor today:

Me and Montana C.

Kid who did all the talking and explaining about it:

Montana C.

Kid who just stood up there:

Me.

Teacher who raised one eyebrow and looked not so impressed with the silent kid:

Mr. Leonard.

Kid who made Mr. Leonard smile with his explanation of his map:

Noah.

What he explained:

The only thing on this imaginary ocean floor is a massive Sloane's viperfish. Because the Sloane's viperfish ate up every other thing that was ever there before.

—⁓⁓—

October 23, Saturday

Dad sure loves when our team wins.

Mom said, "But what we're really proud of is how well you all worked together and had fun and were good sports, win OR lose."

Dad said, "Absolutely."

But when Mom turned around to see what Elizabeth was screaming about, Dad danced around whisper-singing, "We won! We won! We won like winning winners, yo!"

And then he stopped as soon as Mom looked at him.

And then started again.

Again and again.

—⁓—

October 24, Sunday

<u>*In Our Family We Don't Criticize in Front of Others.*</u>

Except today Mom broke that rule.

Yes. Mom. And I'm not even talking about when she said, "Stop asking me about a scooter, Justin, or you'll never get one in your entire life." Because that kerfuffle was just in front of me.

Gingy and Poopsie were over for dinner when she got an e-mail from Elizabeth's teacher, who was requesting a meeting with Mom and Dad because of what has been going on with Elizabeth and Buckey. Which reminded me, I still haven't found out if his real name is Bucket. But I didn't get to bring up that question because Mom asked Elizabeth, "What has been going on with you and Buckey?"

"Nothing," Elizabeth said, concentrating very much on twirling her spaghetti.

"Why does your teacher want to meet with us about it then?" Dad asked.

"Oh, probably because I kissed him. It was no big deal."

Everybody wanted more information about THAT, including Qwerty.

But Elizabeth said, "I don't kiss and tell."

Mom and Dad wanted to know where she ever heard such an expression. She wouldn't answer that, either.

I have a theory. I think it was somebody who whispered, "Atta girl" to Elizabeth and then kissed his wife whose name is Gingy and said, "I don't kiss and tell either."

—⁓—

October 25, Monday

For homework we have to write what we are going to be when we grow up. For the Halloween celebration on Friday, which is not actually Halloween, we are supposed to come in dressed as ourselves as grown-ups, to show our jobs. I think we should be allowed to keep our options open about our careers for a little while longer, but apparently by fourth grade it is time to make some choices and commit. Elizabeth used to want to be a Vegetarian as her job. Last month she wanted to be a Ninja. Now she wants to be President and a Part-Time Ninja and also a Firefighter and a Lobster and a Flower-Picker, but mostly she wants to stop getting put in trouble for kissing Buckey.

"I have a lot of ambitions, Justin," she told me.

I was thinking I would steal *Ninja* but we have to write down WHY we want to be it and I don't have a good reason. I don't think Mr. Leonard would accept *Because ninjas are cool.*

So instead of playing video games with Poopsie like I want to, I have to sit here at my desk, trying to think of a good reason why I want to be Qwerty (or I could just say a Dog) when I grow up.

The actual reason, which I can't write down obviously, is:

Because that is such a good costume, so gluey and toilet-papery.

—*mmm*—

October 26, Tuesday

WHEN I GROW UP

By Justin K., 4-L

I want to be a Philanthropist when I grow up. The reason I want to be a Philanthropist is because those guys are all rich. Every single one. You can't say the same for all baseball players or all businessmen or all rock stars, only Philanthropists. So *therefore*, that is the job that I choose. Philanthropist. *Also*, part of your job if you are a Philanthropist is: They name stuff after you like hospitals and Bowl games and sometimes a stadium. That would be okay with me. My grandfather suggested this occupation to me, *although* he is a retired cobbler, which means either: a kind of pie or you repair shoes. He was the type of cobbler with shoes, according to his wife, who is probably the more reliable source because I don't think Type of Pie is a job even if Poopsie says *Oh, yes, it was, back in The Day. Things have changed a lot. Kids these days.*

But *anyway*, Poopsie recommends Philanthropist over Cobbler as a job so I will go with that. I would like to make shoes, I think, or even repair them because I like tools (the regular kind that go in a box, I mean, not transition words, no offense), but I do not enjoy pie. (No offense if you like pie.)

I was thinking maybe I would like to be a Ninja, *however*, Poopsie said it's hard to make a living these days as a Ninja. I told him well, that's a drawback because I would like to be a Billionaire. Or possibly a Trillionaire. Poopsie thought that was a good idea, being something with "aire" at the end of it. He said you end up very wealthy in those fields.

In conclusion, since Gingy said that Billionaire and Trillionaire are not jobs, try again before I will give either of you knuckleheads a snack, Poopsie and I decided I should be a Philanthropist.

The End.

By Justin Krzeszewski

October 27, Wednesday

On Friday we have to come to school dressed up as our job that we want. Too bad I forgot about being a Lumberjack because if I wrote that, I could wear jeans and a flannel shirt like Cash. Lumberjacks are The Boss. The Boss means the coolest and you can't criticize it at all, in Cash language. Instead now I am going to have to wear my suit and instead of like a Boss, I will look like what I want to be when I grow up is Bartholomew Wiggins.

October 28, Thursday

Noah says Philanthropist is not a job.

Yeah?

Well, Gastroenterologist is not a job, Noah. It's a kind of sea creature, I bet. That's what Gianni Schicci said, anyway, and maybe he doesn't know very much about things other than cheating and being a goofball, but I think on this one he might be right.

Even if he is dressing up as a Pirate tomorrow, which I don't think is a real job either. But he gets to bring a sword and wear an eye patch, so that's way cooler than something that sounds like probably it's the loser cousin of an octopus and too bad if that makes Noah sad on the playground when people say that.

He shouldn't have laughed at my job choice. That is probably even a school rule he broke, laughing at me like that. But is he the one who ends up in the Principal's Office?

No.

That would be my little sister, the Kissing Bandit.

—*un*—

October 29, Friday

If we all succeed at our ambitions, there are going to be a

lot of sports stars in the future who went to
W. H. Taft Elementary School. Plus a
Lumberjack, a Gastroenterologist,
a President (Montana C.), some
Teachers (a lot of the girls and
some of the boys, who all basically
dressed up as Mr. Leonard), a
Pirate, a Geologist (Bartholomew
Wiggins), a Cat (Montana B., who I
think didn't get a good
grade on this), a Movie
Director (Daisy), and a
Computer Genius/LEGO
Designer/Video-Game-Maker
(Xavier Schwartz, who just
spray-painted his hair green as
his costume).
We had to stand up and
say our names and our jobs in
the morning assembly. And then spend the
whole day in our costumes. Ms. Zhang said
she thought mine was hilarious. Mr. Calabrio

didn't seem so impressed, but since I had on shoes instead of sneakers I was excused from playing lacrosse, so I didn't mind. Even though I had to sit next to Penelope Ann Murphy, who wants to be a ballet dancer, the kind who stands on her tiptoes all day. She got excused too because she could barely walk in those things, never mind run. She stole them from her mom's closet, she told me.

Good thing I didn't say Detective for my thing or I might have to turn her in to the authorities for robbery.

October 30, Saturday

I told Mom instead of the police on Penelope Ann Murphy.

I swore Mom to secrecy before I told her, while we were walking Qwerty.

Mom said it was good I told her, but Penelope's mother had probably figured it out already.

What I do not want to be when I grow up:

A Tattletale.

Maybe I should also have told Mom about all the mean stuff Noah has been doing lately too, so she could be proud of me for using words instead of fists again, and also for understanding that maybe Noah is having a hard year, and for being patient and a good friend to him. It makes me feel very excellent when she says stuff like that. It's nice to hear from her about how good I am. It almost takes the stinger out of the Noah meannesses.

But it was time to leave for soccer, so I didn't have time. I dressed up as a soccer player in the horrible cleats that we have to wear this year, and I pretended to be a sports star.

As a soccer player, I think I am a pretty good Doughnut Eater.

Noah didn't even show up for the game. If he doesn't feel like it, his mom lets him skip.

—⁓⁓—

October 31: HALLOWEEN, Sunday

Because it was weirdly warm out, Mom didn't make us wear jackets over our costumes. I think Elizabeth would have taken hers off and left it in the bushes if Mom had insisted.

"That girl is sure full of beans," Gingy said.

"Reminds me of you," Poopsie said.

They were dressed up for Halloween too, even though they aren't kids. Their costume was Grandparents.

Gingy was dressed as Poopsie and Poopsie was dressed as Gingy.

They should have won for Best Costumes. Everybody thought so. But they didn't. There was a party at Montana C.'s house, and this year everybody was invited, the whole grade, even boys. And parents and siblings and grandparents or whoever. It was in Montana C.'s backyard. There were relay games and jumping on the trampoline (no swords or other props allowed) and sushi and sandwiches cut into triangles.

At 6:30 there was the costume parade and everybody got to vote by secret ballot. Only kids were included in the parade is why Gingy and Poopsie didn't win, I am pretty sure.

Daisy won for girl, which she totally deserved, because her costume was so awesome and she made it completely by herself. She was a daisy. So that was perfect. Elizabeth was disappointed that her Ninja costume didn't win and was working up a full-out pout until Buckey said, "Well, probably if it had blood, you'da won." Elizabeth smiled at that and then kissed Buckey on the cheek. Everybody saw. Dad grabbed her away because, my goodness, how many times does that girl need to learn the rule *No Kissing?*

Cash won for boy, for Lumberjack. I'm not saying that's lame, recycling a costume from a school project. I was dressed as a Philanthropist (which I had to explain at Every Single Door when we trick-or-treated after. All the grown-ups thought I was a Butler or a Fancy Man). But still, if recycled costumes were going to win, I really think the trophy should have gone to Noah.

I do not know how he got that Sloane's viperfish onto his head or how he could see out the mouth with those big teeth blocking his view.

"Yours is definitely the best," I said to Noah.

"Yeah?"

"You're a total boss."

He tilted his head, like he was considering how to respond, but that made it look like the Sloane's viperfish was swimming diagonally toward me. Like a really scary demented predator.

"That means it's awesome," I told him.

"What?" Noah's voice echoed like a villain's inside the fish's body.

"Yikes, Noah!" I yelled. "If you move your head like that, it looks like you're swimming all crazed and hungry!"

Noah wiggled his head back and forth. "Like this?"

"Yes!!!"

The other kids came over.

"Check this out," I said. "Is that the most awesome thing ever?"

"Totally!" Xavier Schwartz yelled.

"Youch!" Gianni Schicci screamed, running away. "It's gonna eat me!"

"Chase him," I whispered to Noah.

So Noah did, and we all chased Noah because we were also, in addition to being Pirates and

Ninjas and Flowers and Philanthropists, a big gang of Sloane's Viperfish Hunters.

It was even better than the two full-size candy bars I got from trick-or-treating later, plus the fun-size peanut-butter cup Noah gave me without even making me trade him for it.

November 1, Monday

I do not mind being late to school, even when it means Mom has to write a note and walk me and Elizabeth in through quiet empty corridors, with Mom's shoes clicking, and mine and Elizabeth's squeaking. I don't mind standing at the desk in the Front Office, waiting for a Late Pass while Ms. Robitel behind the desk frowns at me, her glasses way down at the very tip of her nose. At least I got to miss Recorder and the spelling test.

What I do mind is having no more Halloween candy to choose a piece a day from all month.

The reason I have no candy on only November 1 is:
Somebody who didn't need a costume to be a big drooly dog for Halloween gobbled up everything from my trick-or-treat bag.

And then puked it all over the living room.

And then came crying, loudly ashamed, to my bed to wake me up.

I also did mind helping Dad clean it up as punishment because why didn't I put my bag away in a kitchen cabinet? I tried to explain that I always leave it on my floor, every year before this. I didn't know the rules have changed since we got a dog.

But they have changed and I'm in trouble, double trouble for not knowing that fact, I guess.

I would be so mad at the person who came up with the let's-get-a-dog idea if that person's name were not Justin Case.

Things I Am Good at Getting:

   2. In trouble

―᚜᚜᚜―

November 2, Tuesday

The new rule at recess is we don't get free play. Today we had to play Wiffle ball. I was feeling kind of down in the dumps about that because my favorite sport is Just Playing and recess is the one time you get for that. Noah and I were sitting next to each other, waiting to be up.

"This stinks," I said.

"Yeah," Noah said. He gave me one of the fun-size candy bars he had in his pocket from his Halloween bag, since he

doesn't have a dog. He kept the Krackle for himself and gave me the Special Dark, but still, it was fairly generous.

I don't know how many fun-size candy bars are in a serving.

Mostly it was nice, just sitting there like that. A lot of the other kids were cheering and stuff, but me and Noah were just sitting there down in the dumps together.

November 3, Wednesday

Noah is going to run for class representative on the *Bring Back Free Play at Recess* platform.

Cash is going to run on the *I'm Cash* platform.

I have a feeling I know which way this thing is going to go.

November 4, Thursday

I was up at bat, wishing a hole would please open up all around home plate and I could please fall into it before Xavier Schwartz threw another ball right past my face. And before Cash could yell again, "SWING, JUSTIN CASE! SWING!"

No luck. No hole for me.

Strike two.

I was just sick of standing there, waiting to strike out or walk and I guess still mad about the lack of free play, so I swung. I was thinking, *It's so unfair*, after we had Recorder (new song: "Three Blind Mice") and then a spelling test (I think I might have put too many *h*'s in *rhythm*), and then long division with Show Your Work. We should be able to play. Just play.

POP

So I swung the bat and swatted that ball far away. That's how mad I was.

"Run! Run, Justin Case! Run!"

"Whoa! What a hit!"

I was still just standing there, annoyed about the lack-of-recess, while everybody on my team was yelling that.

But then I was like, *Wait, WHAT?*

Because Gianni Schicci was running way far away, toward the jungle gym, chasing the Wiffle ball I'd hit so hard. And my team was yelling FOR me, not AT me.

I ran. I touched first base with the toe of my sneaker and then, since they were still yelling RUN!, I turned left and ran some more. I stopped on second base. I stood on top of the base and rested with my hands on my knees.

"Awesome hit!" Cash yelled toward me.

I smiled back.

Montana B. was up next. She got out and recess ended.

Everybody high-fived me as we walked back in, and said stuff like "What a shot!" and "NICE!"

I put my hand up for a high five from Noah. He hit it so hard, my hand almost got knocked clean off my wrist. I am pretty sure he meant it in a good way.

But not 100 percent sure.

———

November 5, Friday

Mom said I could have one friend over to help me help at Elizabeth's birthday party next week. I was thinking of inviting

Cash. Or maybe Montana C. or Daisy, but they are girls, and probably Xavier Schwartz is too wild. And Gianni Schicci is too weird. He's been walking around beeping, pretending to be a robot, a lot lately.

Cash would be fun, but I thought Noah would really like it if I asked him and, anyway, he's known Elizabeth practically her whole life. And he's feeling worried about the election. He says no, he's not worried. He says he knows he's going to win. He thinks the *Bring Back Free Play at Recess* platform is a Can't Lose platform. Who would vote against that?

I know a lot about worries, so I can tell he actually is worried though.

Anyway, maybe Cash would think it was boring to help at a first-grader's party. Or maybe he would think, *Why would Justin Case invite ME?*

So I chose Noah.

Elizabeth's party is right before Class Rep elections, so the other thing is, Noah might be happy for the distraction, I think. Last year, when I was running for class rep, my favorite thing to think about was:

Anything Else.

I hope I don't regret choosing Noah the way I regret not wearing my rain jacket today. It is so annoying when Mom is right about the weather.

―――

November 6, Saturday

I played goalie in the second half of the soccer game. The nice part of that was the free time. It was relaxing, because I could mostly just stand there enjoying the afternoon while everybody else was running around like mosquitoes.

The not-so-nice part was when suddenly everybody and the ball were all charging fast toward me.

Luckily, Sam Pasternak is huge and strong and he most of the time kicked that ball away. But twice it got by him. Unluckily.

The first time it sailed into the other side of the net from where I was standing. One for the Raging Tigers, tying up the score. I watched the backs of my teammates slump away from me.

Nobody even said, *That's okay, Justin Case.* Or *Good try.*

Or *Hang in there.*

Not even my dad, over on the sidelines. He was very busy looking at his shoes.

The other time, I watched the ball come off the foot of the biggest kid on the Raging Tigers and zoom, in slow motion, right toward me. I wasn't thinking about trying to make an awesome brave block. I wasn't even thinking of how to escape. I was just watching the ball come toward me closer and closer. If I was thinking anything, it was: *Oh, no, oh, no.*

Then *boom*, there I was on the ground. I felt like a Colonial guy getting hit by a cannonball.

When I could open my eyes, I noticed there was a soccer ball where my belly used to be.

"Awesome," Sam yelled, lifting me up.

"What a block!" Cash yelled, thumping me on the back.

I didn't say anything because I couldn't. My body had changed into a capital *C*.

On the way home, after we'd won 2–1, Dad bragged to Mom and Elizabeth that I may have found my calling as a soccer player: Goalie.

Still, I think I might stick with either Philanthropist or Lumberjack as a job. Although I do like the after-game praise and doughnut portion of a soccer star's life.

November 7, Sunday

The Stuffties on my bed have been excluding Snakey. They are accusing him of being too scary. I understand why they would want to do that, but I am not sure it is nice. Or smart.

Snakey is spending a lot of time coiled up at the end of the bed, maybe cooking up some evil kerfuffles against the others. Or maybe he's just napping. It is sometimes hard to tell with stuffties.

—mm—

November 8, Monday

I am so mad at Mom, I feel like I completely *no, thank you* her.

No. You know what? Hate.

They can't make me not think it in the privacy of my own brain. *Hate. Hate hate hate.*

I wish I could draw *X*s on all her shirts.

It is scary to feel like this, but I actually mean it.

—mm—

November 9, Tuesday

Penelope Ann Murphy's mom and my mom are two of the moms who all had coffee together, and somehow my mom told

Penelope Ann Murphy's mom about Penelope stealing the ballet toe shoes out of her closet.

After Mom promised she would never tell that secret I told her about those dumb toe shoes.

Mom said she didn't remember saying anything specific about Penelope Ann Murphy stealing the toe shoes. But she looked a little worried about why was I asking her that question.

"What exactly did you tell Penelope Ann Murphy's mom?" I asked her.

"Justin, I don't remember exactly."

"Fine! Approximately!"

"I just, I didn't . . ." Mom said, looking at her wiggling toes on the floor.

"Mom!"

"Well, I remember Mrs. Murphy talking about it, and all the moms were laughing. . . ."

"Laughing?" I asked.

"Mrs. Murphy is a good storyteller, and . . ." She reached for my hand, but I pulled it away. "I don't remember saying anything, really."

"What do you mean, anything really?" I yelled.

"Maybe Mrs. Murphy figured out what happened to the toe shoes by herself?" Mom suggested.

"No!" I yelled. "She didn't!"

"Justin, I . . ."

"You must have told her, because Penelope Ann Murphy came into school and yelled at me in front of everybody for telling on her!"

"Oh, no," Mom said.

"Oh, yes!" I yelled. "A huge kerfuffle!"

"A huge . . . what?"

"Kerfuffle! Kerfuffle! Don't you even know what *kerfuffle* means?" I realized right then that kerfuffle is one of those words that sounds very silly when you say it too many times in a row, but it was too late. "It was a huge kerfuffle, I mean it, Mom! It's not funny! And what could I even say? Because I did tell on her! To you!"

"I'm so sorry, Justin," Mom said. She tried to cuddle me up but I was feeling about as cuddly as a Sloan's viperfish or maybe a bullhead shark.

"Justin," Mom called after me while I stomped up to my room. "Justin, come back."

I didn't. She might be sorry, but she is not the one everybody in fourth grade is calling the horrible name of Tattletale. She is not the one who had to work independently on the science project yesterday and today when even Noah was included. She was not the one who Noah leaned in close to at recess and whispered, "Why would you tell on Penelope Ann Murphy?"

Nope. That wasn't Mom. That was me.

———

November 10, Wednesday

At lunch Noah was sitting squished in between Cash and Xavier Schwartz. When I went over nobody made room for me. I stood there for a long minute, behind all my friends, holding my lunch bag, waiting for a spot. No one looked up, even when I said, "Hey." No one budged even when I said, "Can I . . . get in here? Somewhere?"

So I had to make the long walk down to the deserted end of the table and sit down all alone.

My cheese sandwich tasted like an old sponge waiting by the side of the sink to get thrown in the garbage.

Instead of going out to play at recess, I went for extra recorder work. The only other kid there was Penelope Ann Murphy. She had hate darts firing out of her eyes at me the whole time. Maybe I improved a little at smooth airy breath skills, but at my level of recorder terribleness, it is hard to notice.

After school Noah came home with me to help with Elizabeth's birthday party. He acted like nothing was wrong, like he hadn't ignored me all day. He smiled at me like he and I were best friends all during the party, while we were setting up Pin the Sword on the Ninja and handing out slices of pizza.

"I'm so mad at my mom," I whispered to him while we waited at the front door with loot bags at the end of the party. "I wish I could put HER in trouble."

"Your mom?"

"Uh-huh."

"Put your mom in trouble?"

"Yes. She promised she wouldn't tell Penelope Ann Murphy's mom what I told her and then . . ."

"Guess it runs in your family," Noah said. "Telling what you promise not to, I mean."

That didn't cheer me up at all.

"You were right about Cash, though," he said, stealing a candy from one of the loot bags. "He really is fun."

I just nodded.

November 11, Thursday

There was no school for Veterans Day. Phew. I really needed the break. And I don't just mean so I could learn how to spell those crazy things on this week's list, like *weird* and *science* and *friend*.

I kept getting that last one wrong until Dad said, "Just remember that FRIEND has the word END in it."

Now I will never forget that one. That is for sure.

November 12, Friday

In art class, while we were all trying to weave our Colonial pot holders, Penelope Ann Murphy told the tragedy of being tattled on by me again. She was starting to cry, of course. I tried to concentrate on my pot holder, even though I did not care at all about my pot holder or weaving or even Colonial Times very much.

"And he just, he tattled on me," Penelope Ann Murphy was saying. "And I got punished—no screen time for two weeks!" I could hear the tears in her voice.

"Oh, enough already," Montana C. mumbled. "Old news."

"I'm still punished," Penelope Ann Murphy said, sniffling.

"Yeah, well. Guess what." Montana C. slammed her half-made Colonial pot holder down onto the art table. "You stole your mother's stuff and then you denied it when she asked you about it. Of course you got punished. Leave Justin Case out of it and move the heck on."

I tried to hold my smile in, but it might not have been a completely successful hide.

At lunch I went straight to the lonely end of the lunch table. As bad as it felt down there, it wasn't as awful as standing behind people hoping they'd make a space for me. Noah was sitting between Xavier and Cash again. I don't know what he was saying, but I heard Cash say, "Ew, Noah! Give it a break! Not while we're eating, dude!"

"Yeah," all the other boys said.

I was staring at my sandwich, wishing there were such a thing as *Veterans Day 2: You Get Friday Off Also*, when Montana C. sat down next to me. She didn't say anything, just took her sandwich and water bottle out. Then Daisy came over and joined us. And a bunch of the other girls.

It felt like I'd wandered into the wrong bathroom.

But it was nice of them.

Cash came and stood next to me while I was on deck for baseball at after-lunch recess. I stopped swinging the bat so I wouldn't accidentally knock his head off his neck. I wasn't planning to swing at the ball so I didn't need the practice.

"I really stink at baseball," I said.

"Nah, you're okay," he said. "So why did you tell on Penelope Ann Murphy, anyway?"

"I didn't really," I said. "Well, I didn't mean to. I was just talking about it with my mom, not to get her put in trouble or anything."

"No?"

"No! I mean, Penelope Ann Murphy told me she stole the toe shoes. It felt like, I don't know, aren't you supposed to tell a grown-up if somebody tells you they committed a crime? Isn't that like a rule or something?"

"Yeah, probably," Cash said. "Good point."

"So," I said. "That's why."

"A lot of kids would've just denied telling their mom. Blamed somebody else."

I shrugged at that.

"It's cool you didn't."

I didn't say, *Maybe I would have if I'd thought of that idea.* Instead I nodded a little, like Cash does, slow and with squinted eyes.

"You're up," he said. I got walked, and then Cash hit a blast almost into the woods, so we both scored.

I got 100 percent on my spelling test, which was also nice. Even though the spelling trick Dad taught me makes my heart feel like somebody was just swinging his arm and punched me right in it.

November 13, Saturday

Soccer got canceled. Rain. Hallelujah.

And then another hallelujah happened: Cash called to ask if I wanted to go to the movies with him and Xavier Schwartz this afternoon. His mom could pick me up before and drop me off after.

I said, "Hold on. I'll ask."

Mom said yes. And she let me not take an umbrella, so no risk of it pinching off my finger in the closey mechanism, and also she let me wear my fleece, like all the other boys wear when it rains, instead of my rain slicker even though it was still raining.

I was a little bit happy for the first time all week.

November 14, Sunday

A thing Cash said yesterday that I keep thinking about:

It's one thing when you are in second or third grade. But by the time you're in fourth, you can't just let your feelings out in school.

I am 95 percent sure we were still talking about Penelope Ann Murphy. She was crying again on Friday on the way to music about getting in trouble for stealing her mother's ballet shoes. Everybody, definitely including me, agreed that the trouble she got put in for that was ancient history, get over it. Enough already. She was just trying to keep getting attention and sympathy for old news.

I am 3 percent sure, though, that maybe I let my feelings out in school sometimes without meaning to, and Cash was giving me the advice too.

And I am 2 percent just completely unsure of everything in general, including whether the stuff we put on the popcorn was melted butter like Xavier Schwartz said it definitely was, even though the dispenser did not say butter, it said "Golden Flavor." Which does not sound like food, or even a flavor.

November 15, Monday

The election for Class Rep is tomorrow. Noah wore his suit today and kept trying to shake hands with everybody while asking for their vote. There were no campaign managers allowed this year. But if I had been Noah's campaign manager, I would have said the advice of:

Maybe stop trying to shake everybody's hand so much.

And also:

We already know your name, Noah. We have known you since kindergarten, so you really don't need to keep saying, *Hello, my name is Noah and I am running for Class Rep.*

We already know. Seriously. We know.

But when I tried to get him to play Tag with everybody in our five minutes of Free Play Mr. Calabrio let us have because of the such nice weather, Noah growled at me and then kept right on introducing himself to all the kids who already know him and were just trying to play Tag in the sunshine.

Our spelling words for the week are all "tion" words. *Election, selection, elation, rejection.*

Mr. Leonard might be choosing those exact words because he magically knows exactly which thoughts are in our heads.

Maybe he really is an Alien Mind Reader. A lot of kids think he actually is. And everything he says and does proves it.

Like today, before dismissal, he gave us the speech about how Class Rep Election is not a popularity contest.

True, every teacher every year gives that same speech. But all the kids who take the school bus home from 4-L think that when that left eyebrow of Mr. Leonard's went up, he was really saying the opposite. Like he was really saying:

I know it is a popularity contest.

And I know who is going to win.

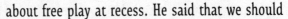

November 16, Tuesday

Noah wore his suit again and wrote his speech on index cards but also memorized it. It was a good speech. It was all

about free play at recess. He said that we should have it even in bad weather because it is important to our education, according to many studies, and in addition it is our right.

Everybody clapped when he was done. Noah smiled really big and bowed a little before heading back to his seat.

Cash just wore his regular stuff and didn't have notes. He went up to the front of the room, to the space where Noah had been standing, and waited with his hands in his jeans pockets for a few seconds, not like he was scared, but just calm, just enjoying the moment or something. Like he was about to blow out the candles on his perfect birthday cake.

Then he smiled a tiny bit, just one side of his mouth, ducked his head, and said:

> Well, I'm Cash, as you know. And I'm not going to
> promise any big changes I will make in Student
> Government. I don't know if they'd listen, even,
> and I don't like to make promises I can't surely
> keep. So. Well. Mostly I just want to thank
> everybody for being so cool to me. It's kind of
> terrifying, you know, being the new kid.
> But you guys made me feel like,
> well, like a new friend, but
> like a new friend who will
> someday be your old friend.
> Which is awesome of you.
> So. Thanks.

Everybody clapped.

Then we had to put our heads down on our desks and close our eyes. My desk smelled like paste. I breathed it in, hoping paste is not a poisonous smell, while Mr. Leonard said Noah's name and then Cash's name. With our faces hidden in the triangles of our left arms, we had to decide when to raise our right hands. Right after the name of the kid we wanted to represent us. Only one hand-raise per person.

"Thank you," Mr. Leonard said. "I will post the results while you are out."

So we all went to for recess. We were forced to play lacrosse the whole time. We stunk. Nobody could concentrate. Even the sporty kids kept dropping the ball. I was not worse than anyone at lacrosse (except Montana C.) for once.

When we came in from recess, Mr. Leonard's clear script on the board said:

Class Rep for 4-L: Cash Plotz

A few kids were congratulating Cash. Noah didn't even sit down. He stood in the classroom doorway with his face getting redder and his eyes getting wetter and his hand raised. Mr. Leonard was busy giving a speech about how close the vote was and how well the campaigns were run and how many other opportunities there are to serve the school community.

Finally he called on Noah, who asked, "May I please go to the bathroom? Right away. Please."

When I showed up in the bathroom ten minutes later, it was only because Mr. Leonard sent me to see if Noah was okay in there. I could hear kids giggling as I left the classroom, but I ignored that. That's what Mom and Mr. Leonard both say you should do if somebody is giggling at you in an unkind way.

Noah was in a stall, crying. I heard him. It wasn't the quiet type of crying.

"Mr. Leonard wanted . . ." I said.

"Get out!" Noah yelled.

"Okay." I said. I started to go, but then I thought, *Well, maybe I should hang out for a minute*, in case he needed a friend. "Noah?"

"I said leave me alone!"

"I'll tell Mr. Leonard you'll be back soon, okay?"

"I don't care," he said inside the stall.

"I'm sure it really was close," I told him. "Very close. Like Mr. Leonard said."

"Did you vote for me?" he asked me.

"Yes," I said.

He blew his nose and then whispered, "Thanks, Justin."

—⁓—

November 17, Wednesday

But that was a lie.

—⁓—

November 18, Thursday

Noah was absent. For pinkeye.

And he doesn't have any brothers, so if it is true, what everybody was saying about how you get pinkeye, I am not sure what happened to him or where or how.

There were a lot of theories going around. None of them nice.

—⁓—

November 19, Friday

You don't get pinkeye from farts.

That is the one thing I learned in school today, and now I

(and everybody in 4-L except Noah who was absent again) have to write one full page, over the weekend, about what pinkeye is, how you get it for real, and how to prevent it.

Mr. Leonard invited Ms. Khan the School Nurse to come in to be a guest in our classroom, to explain what an infection is and what pinkeye is, and also why people pass gas.

Grown-ups should not talk about farts, no matter what they call it, if they want fourth-graders to maintain control of ourselves.

—*mm*—

November 20, Saturday

Things I Am Good at Getting:

3. Pinkeye.

I hate everybody.

And everything.

—*mm*—

November 21, Sunday

I especially hate Noah, farts, kerfuffles, bathrooms that I am sent to when I didn't even want to go, and eyes.

And pink. Stupid pink. What kind of color even is that? Light red? Add white to blue and do you have to give it its own dumb name? No. It's just light blue. Light green. Light yellow. But with red? *Pink.*

I hate colors that need their own special treatment.

Also, ointment. Ew. Is that stuff just intentionally disgusting? To punish people who have pinkeye? To make them blinder and *sadder*? The guy who invented ointment should have to live in ointment for the rest of his life.

Jerk.

—*mm*—

November 22, Monday

In May, we will have Fourth-Grade Tests, which count. On them we will have to write an essay. So we have to get started on practicing doing that right away, even though it is only November, so who even knows if May will ever come. "That's like predicting the future," Xavier Schwartz said. But it doesn't matter. Tomorrow during school we will have to write an essay about something we are thankful for.

For homework tonight we just have to write a good long list of what we are thankful for, and then tomorrow in school we will choose one, only one, to write about.

Things I Am Thankful For:

1. That pinkeye goes away fast.

2.

—*mm*—

November 23, Tuesday

WHAT I AM THANKFUL FOR

By Justin K., 4-L

A thing that I am thankful for is my friends. Who aren't a thing, but you know what I mean with that Topic Sentence.

(Mr. Leonard, I really wish we could be allowed to use pencil for first drafts *because* I keep messing up and it comes out not saying exactly what I mean or it sounds better in my head. It's kind of, like, I get going on one path of thinking and I can't remember what I was going to say, but it's too late. Anyway, if you could from now on please say okay to pencils for drafts so we can erase the mess-ups without it looking like just a big bruise of ink on the page, I would be thankful for THAT. I would even write a whole new essay on my thankfulness of Now We Can Write in Pencil. And you wouldn't have to give me extra credit for it. Unless you want to. ☺ Thank you. Back to the essay now.)

So anyway, about my friends. Well, I am thankful that they like me. Most of the time. I think they like me. Hmm. If they don't like me, wow. That would stink. What if they don't like me?

I Am Thankful is the topic, though. So:

I am thankful that my friends are usually pretty good at fooling me that they do like me, if they don't. Hahahaha.

Really, an eraser would be a top thankful thing for me right now.

My friends *include* (I am not sure if *include* is a transition word *because* I know *including* is, but *whatever*) Noah, Cash, Xavier Schwartz, *and also* some girls, *even though* they are girls, *for example* Daisy and Montana C. They are my friends because they are fun to play with and are just, you know, nice. (Not just the girls. The boys too.) *Also*

Gianni Schicci was nice after a disaster (caused by him *but* still) last year, *but* he is in the other class *so* you probably don't know him and I don't do that much stuff with him this year. *Plus* he cheats, *so* it's annoying sometimes to play with him, *but* maybe he's growing out of that.

I am thankful that these friends of mine are fun and funny (not just bathroom humor *but also* other kinds) *and* usually don't punch me in the stomach *except* sometimes Noah who swings his arm a lot when my belly is near him. I think maybe Noah is having a hard year this year. I am trying to be patient and understanding, *but* it is not always easy. Noah and I have been friends since we were in nursery school. I am thankful for that. Cash and I have been friends only since camp. I didn't even know we liked each other that much in camp. I thought we weren't friends, actually, but I was wrong, I guess.

That is a thing to be thankful for too, sometimes, in a weird way, don't you think, Mr.

Leonard? Being thankful about being wrong about something is strange when you think about it a little, but if you think about it a lot it's, like, *Oh, okay.* It is good to be wrong about somebody you thought was rough and maybe even mean but it turns out he's nice. And also, if you thought that kid didn't like you. Like, I thought Cash thought I was not a sporty kid, just a worried kid who should not be included.

I am thankful for being included and having so many friends.

I would be thankful if they all liked to play together more and none of them acted weird. Or sad. Or sometimes mean to me, like not wanting to share Oreos with me just with Bartholomew Wiggins. Or kicking my chair sometimes. *Such as* every time he walks past it.

Also this might be weird, but sometimes it would be good to have fewer friends. Like when you don't know which friend to be thankful to play with at recess that day. Do you know what I mean? Like, imagine it is Tug-of-War and I am the rope. Is how it feels sometimes.

In conclusion, I am thankful you are a teacher who might not take off points for bad spelling (I hope). And also about the friends.

The End

By Justin K.

—

November 24, Wednesday

Mr. Leonard made me stay in during recess because I got a big red *SEE ME* on my thankfulness essay.

In trouble again. Great.

I got all ready with, *Okay, maybe it was a disaster of an essay, but it was very long. I wrote so much and a kid should get some credit for that, at least.*

Mr. Leonard said he wanted to talk about what is going on with me.

I concentrated very much on not crying because I am a fourth-grader so it is not okay to show my feelings in school. The concentrating on not crying made it hard for me to answer Mr. Leonard's questions.

He wanted to know if somebody really has been punching me in the stomach.

I didn't want to tell.

I didn't want to lie.

So I didn't answer. I sat there wishing maybe he had to go to a meeting soon and I could go outside to recess with all the other 4-L kids.

"Justin, please stop shrugging," Mr. Leonard said. "I would really like to hear your thoughts."

So I took a big gulp of air and said, "Noah was just swinging his arm. I was not tattletaling on him. Please don't put him or me in trouble or anybody, please may I please be dismissed?"

Mr. Leonard's head sank a little bit and he looked at his very long fingers, which were cooperating with one another between his knees. The pointers made a triangle together.

"I could write a new essay about being thankful for my dog," I offered. "I am not as scared of him as I used to be. And you wouldn't even have to give me extra credit for it even though it would be an extra essay. Would that be better?"

"Your essay was fine, and you aren't in trouble."

"Phew," I said.

"You seem a little worried."

"Nope," I said. "Me? Worried? HA!"

BOTH of Mr. Leonard's eyebrows went up at that. Maybe he was startled by the loudness of the HA! We looked at each other with hugely open eyes while the HA! faded slowly away in the air.

Afterward I explained, more quietly, "I used to be a very worried kid. I am not a worried kid anymore. But maybe there's a little left over. Like a stain."

Mr. Leonard smiled. "Well," he said, "you can always talk to me about whatever's going on. Remember that. And it doesn't have to be tattletaling to talk with an adult if something or someone is bothering you. Okay?"

"Okay," I said, and then he let me go out to recess.

It was so late in recess and the game was already going, so I just got to sit on the grass. I leaned back on my elbows, looked at the cumulus clouds drifting by, and wasn't in trouble.

Which I am very thankful for.

—*m*—

November 25, Thursday

More Things I Am Thankful For:

1. Apple pie AND blueberry pie, AND you can just eat the crust, leave the goo, AND you don't have to have pumpkin pie.

2. Hide-and-Seek with cousins.

3. Vacation.

4. Extra grandparents named Ninny and Bop who are visiting from Florida with perfect presents for us even though Thanksgiving is not a present-y holiday, just because they love us.

5. My new scooter, which is exactly the one I was secretly hoping for.

6. Maybe not so secretly.

7. Parents who tell the scooter secret to grandparents.

8. And say okay even if it is dangerous to ride a scooter and you have to wear a helmet every single time *no exceptions, mister.*

9. Little sisters who need to share your hiding spot because they get scared when they hide all alone in Hide-and-Seek with the cousins.

10. Laps of grown-ups who let you fall asleep with your head there while they talk talk talk like a lullaby.

November 26, Friday

I will ride my scooter. I just need to try it alone for the first few times, not with the entire extended family watching. Also it looked like it might start raining. And I needed to play with my Knights, who were having a very big battle, and not just the one against my little cousins Dylan and Dermot, who thought maybe the Knights were chew toys.

Dylan and Dermot are not that much younger than Elizabeth, but maybe she is mature or maybe they have rabies.

Noah told me all about rabies after we got a dog last year and he didn't.

Elizabeth kept trying to explain the rain cycle to everybody. Everybody already knows about the rain cycle. I suggested to Elizabeth that maybe she could explain it to Dylan and Dermot.

That would solve her problem of needing to explain the rain cycle to somebody and, at the same time, solve my problem of STOP TOUCHING MY KNIGHTS YOU HORRIBLES at the same time.

"Do you know where the rain goes after it falls?" she asked them in her sweetest voice, as if they were two years old instead of almost five and almost six.

"On the ground," Dylan said, poking Dermot with my Knight named Aesop Fable.

"On the ground, on the ground, on the ground," Dermot repeated, throwing my Knight named Dragon Green Walker at Dylan's head.

"Ow!" Dylan yelled, poking Dermot with Achilles Heel's already-wobbly sword.

I unwound their sticky little fingers from my Knights as quickly as

I could. "Let's put these away," I said for, like, the hundredth time. "These are not for little . . ."

"We're not little!" Dermot shrieked.

"Not little!!!" Dylan also shrieked. "We are enormous!"

"We are MONSTERS!" Dermot said.

"Well," I said. "True."

"After that," Elizabeth insisted, getting between them. "Guess what happens to the rain! It evaporates!"

"Me no care," Dylan said, stabbing her with Knights as fast as he could grab them away from me.

"And then," Elizabeth said, squeezing Dylan's fists in hers, "after it evaporates, it condensates!"

"Ow," Dylan said.

"It condensifies!" Elizabeth yelled.

"Me have no idea what she talking about," Dermot said, and clonked her on the head with the empty bucket that used to have my Knights in it.

Dylan chased Dermot out of my room.

"I hate kids," Elizabeth said to me.

November 27, Saturday

The cousins and their parents had left after dinner last night so the house was nice and quiet when we woke up. Elizabeth and I snuck down to the living room to try to watch as many cartoons as possible before Mom and Dad woke up.

Ninny and Bop were sitting in the chairs reading sections of the newspaper when we got there.

So we flopped down on the floor, feeling sad about grown-ups who wake up early even on Saturdays.

"What are you learning in school?" Bop asked us.

"The Rain Cycle," Elizabeth said, into the rug.

"What is that?" Ninny asked.

"The Rain Cycle," I said, louder. Sometimes grandparents need the volume turned up.

"Right," Bop said. "We heard the words. But what *is* that? An opera?"

"No, it's just rain," Elizabeth said. "Precipitation. Evaporation. Condensation. Begin again. What happens when it rains."

"No way," Ninny said.

Elizabeth looked from Ninny to Bop and back again. "No way . . . what?"

"We have always wondered what happens when it rains," Bop said. He folded the newspaper he'd been reading. "We were just discussing this the other day."

"Yes," Ninny said, all excited. "Bop said to me, 'Hey, Ninny. Where do you think the rain goes after it puddles?' "

We laughed because she did a very good imitation of Bop.

Bop nodded. "And Ninny said, 'I wish I knew.' " He did a very funny imitation of Ninny.

Ninny sat forward on her chair. "This is so exciting."

"Will you explain it to us?" Bop asked Elizabeth.

"Seriously?"

"Well, any way you want to, dear," Ninny said.

So Elizabeth explained it to them. The entire rain cycle. In much more detail than she even knew. In more detail than anybody ever knew about the rain cycle. It took pretty much the whole day, with only short breaks for food.

—————

November 28, Sunday

I went for a scoot-run with Dad and Qwerty early in the morning, using my new scooter. I never noticed before how

many bumps and jiggles there are on the sidewalks around here. Cash and Xavier Schwartz both go straighter on theirs than I can on mine. Maybe they have better scooters.

But I decided not to give up on scooting yet. I will keep practicing. Dad liked that attitude very much. Much better apparently than the first three attitude options I tried out, which are called Whining, Complaining, and Giving Up.

In the afternoon we went to get the trophies for soccer.

The dad behind us kept grumbling that it's so silly that everybody gets a trophy just for participating. "Makes them soft," he grumbled. "Bunch of hooey."

After about five minutes of that, Dad turned around and said, "That's the goal. The whole goal for right now. Participating!"

"Yeah?" the big dad asked Dad. "When we were kids, you had to achieve something to get a trophy."

"So?" Dad asked. "Lots of stuff is different now. What's the harm if they all get trophies? Come on." He turned around front. Mom put her gentle hand on top of Dad's.

"What's the harm?" the other dad bellowed. He was way bigger than my dad. I scrunched down tight in my chair. "I'll tell you what's wrong with it. Makes them think they'll get trophies just for showing up for the rest of their lives."

"Nope," Dad said, turning around again to face the big red-faced dad. "Not buying it. They're still little kids, all these guys. There's plenty of time for them to learn they won't get trophies every time they show up; that lots of times they won't be the one to get the trophies and the awards. Let's get them to show up first, run around, try. And then we can clap for them. Give them a little shiny something to look at, on top of their dresser, next time they're in their room, thinking maybe it would be a lot easier *not* to show up, *not* to try. You know?"

The dads stared at each other. The girl next to that huge other dad sunk down low in her chair.

"Doesn't hurt anybody to celebrate these kids just showing the heck up," Dad said. "Right?"

"I guess," the other dad grumbled.

Dad turned around to face front again and put his arm around Mom. I was watching his face to see if he looked scared of that big bully dad behind him.

Nope.

I leaned against him a little bit until it was our team's turn to get our glittering gold trophies.

—◆—

November 29, Monday

I was walking in from recess with Cash and Xavier Schwartz, discussing whether Fig Newtons are actually cookies or a secret plot to get kids to eat a vegetable called figs, when Noah bumped into my back.

"Ouch," I said.

Cash and Xavier kept going, still talking about secret plots.

"Just because you walk in from recess with those guys doesn't make you cool," Noah said.

"I didn't say it did," I told him.

"Not in words, maybe," Noah said.

He turned around and walked back outside even though recess was over and you are supposed to go straight in.

I had nobody to walk the rest of the way in with. I let my fingers drag over the cold bumpy wall and just walked to the classroom by myself.

—◆—

November 30, Tuesday

For the holiday concert this year, since we are fourth-graders, we will be singing some songs and also playing our recorders. Thursday in music class they are going to test our voices to see how high and low they go so they can put us into groups.

I don't even like talking in front of the class. Now they want us to sing in front of the whole school and the parents, in high and low voices?

At the same time as we are singing and then playing our recorders and then singing again, we have to stand nicely on the risers and not wiggle, jiggle, or push one another or poke anybody's back with our recorders.

You would think these grown-ups had never met us.

—〰—

December 1, Wednesday

Montana C. says when you wake up on the first day of a new month, you are supposed to say, "Rabbit, rabbit, rabbit," as your first words. If you do, you have good luck all month.

If you don't? Bad luck.

I never heard of that rule before. Everybody else was like, *Yeah, of course, obviously.* I never, in my entire life, said, "Rabbit, rabbit, rabbit," as my first words any day when I woke up.

Which explains a lot.

———

December 2, Thursday

My voice is high.

I stand between Daisy and a whispery girl named Willow who comes up to my armpit. And right behind Montana B., who can't stop bouncing, ever, and whose voice sounds like a baby hamster's.

Cash and Xavier Schwartz and Noah all have low voices. Bartholomew Wiggins has the lowest in fourth grade (of the kids). Only Gianni Schicci of the boys is anywhere near me in the high-voice section, and even he is kind of near some other boys.

Unlike me.

Apparently saying "Rabbit, rabbit, rabbit" as your second thing (after "No, I don't want to get up yet, please five more minutes") on the second day of the month gives you the opposite of good luck.

——

December 3, Friday

It was not my fault I fell down those steps and dropped my books. I would not have fallen if Noah hadn't bumped into me

on our way down, single file and silent, back to our classroom from the science lab.

I know he was mad at not being included in the Taking Care of the Tortoise group. And maybe I should have said to Cash and Xavier that we should ask Noah to be the fourth person in our group. That is what a good friend would do: include his friend.

But Cash said, "Let's see if Montana C. wants in on this."

I was so surprised, I just said, "Yeah."

Also, the thing is, everybody says *yeah* to Cash.

Plus, Montana C. is really good to work in a group with. She works hard and still laughs a lot but not at the wrong times.

And maybe also a small and probably very bad thought mumbled inside my brain:

When I was alone at the lonely end of the lunch table, Noah did not come and sit next to me, did he?

No, he did not. That was Montana C. who came and sat next to me.

For some or maybe all those reasons, I did not say, *Maybe we should ask Noah to join us instead of Montana C.*

Montana C. answered, "Sure, why not?"

I smiled at her and then I turned my face away from Noah's, even though I could feel him looking at me like he wanted to be in our group instead of the one taking care of the tropical fish with Bartholomew Wiggins. So I didn't see Noah's sad eyes.

Except for maybe one second before I stopped seeing them.

I had looked at him with sad eyes in the cafeteria from the far end of the table. And what he did then was, he smiled at me before he turned his face away.

But when Mr. Leonard picked me up by the armpits at the bottom of the stairs and asked, "What happened, young man?" I did not tell on Noah.

"Sorry," I said.

"Gather your things, please, and pay attention as you walk."

"Okay," I said. And I did pay attention to gathering my stuff. What I did not pay attention to was if my friends were laughing at me for falling down the stairs.

Maybe they weren't laughing about that. Maybe somebody had told a really good knock-knock joke and I just hadn't heard it because of being busy with tumbling down those stairs and saying stuff like *OOOF* and *AAAAHHHH*.

But right now, in the dark of my bed, even though I promised three nights in a row on the Pillow of Honor for anyone who could think of one, none of my stuffties can think of any knock-knock jokes that are that funny.

And neither can I.

———

December 4, Saturday

Mom went into Elizabeth's room to have a talk with her. Qwerty and I looked at each other like, *What is going on?* But neither of us had an answer. So he went back to napping and I went back to doing the Battle Between the Forces of Good Knights and Evil Knights.

Mom came storming out of Elizabeth's room right when the Good Guy Knights' castle was being stormed by the Head Bad Guy Knight, Steeltrap. I watched her go, with Steeltrap in one hand and Achilles Heel, the dying Good Guy Knight, in the other hand. Qwerty watched too.

By the time Mom marched back to Elizabeth's room, with Dad right behind her, the tide had turned and the Good Guy Knights were winning.

I wish I knew what Elizabeth is in trouble for, but I was kind of happy nobody was telling me to go outside or clean my room or anything productive all day. I usually like to have a lot of attention, but sometimes I like to have none.

December 5, Sunday

Turns out, Elizabeth is in trouble for *bullying*.

Bullying Buckey.

By keeping trying to kiss him. And he doesn't want her to.

He said, *Please stop,* and *I mean it, Elizabeth, please stop or I am telling*, and she still didn't stop trying to kiss him. So Buckey told the teacher on Elizabeth. And the teacher told Mom

and Dad. They are Very Serious and Elizabeth is in Very Big Trouble. I am not even sure what other punishments she's getting, but I know she was sitting at the kitchen table for a long time writing a letter of apology to Buckey with promises to quit bugging him. And no snacks until she was done.

No smiles, either.

I stayed mostly in my room because Mom and Dad were looking Very Not Smiley, and when I left my sneakers in the slightly wrong place, they said *JUSTIN!* so burstingly I jumped up nearly to the ceiling.

Some new family rules we got today:

No means no.

Use your words, not your kisser.

Put your sneakers away when your sister is in trouble.

Don't be annoying.

--~~~--

December 6, Monday

We had recess right after Music.

Everybody was relieved to get outside even though it was cold and we had to form two lines and wait for Mr. Calabrio to set up relay races.

"We sound awful," Cash said. "Why do they make us play those things anyway?"

"Yeah," I agreed.

"And why do they make us sing such weird stuff?" Xavier asked. "And so many different tunes at once!"

"I have to sing like *lalalala*," I said, imitating how high I have to sing the middle part of the song.

"You sound like a little girl crying when you sing, Justin," Noah said with a huge smile on his huge face. "*Waa waa waa.*" He laughed like he'd just made a hilarious joke. "Justin sounds like a baby girl!"

Montana C. said, "So what? I sound like a boy!"

And then Daisy said, "I sound like a nothing!"

Which made us all (except Noah) laugh. Because Daisy does not sound like a nothing. And also Daisy doesn't usually speak up on the playground.

"Get into two lines!" Mr. Calabrio yelled from the far end of the field. "I'm almost ready!"

"So what if Justin Case sounds like a girl?" Gianni said, putting his face close to Noah's.

"Hey," I said. "I do not sound like a girl! Some boys just have . . ."

"So what, what Justin Case sounds like? Better to sound like a girl than like a fish," Gianni said right in Noah's nose. "You sound like a fish."

"Fish don't sing," Noah said, his face turning bright red like somebody slapped both his cheeks at once. But nobody did. "Fish are silent."

"So why don't you shut up, then, Noah?" Cash said quietly to him. "Come on, Justin." He yanked my sweatshirt sleeve into line in front of him.

"You're not allowed to say *shut up* in school," Noah said from the other line. "It's a rule here, for your information."

"Okay," Cash said, leaning across toward him. "Fine. How about if you try to quiet down now, okay, Noah? Like a fish."

"Well, some aquatic mammals sing," Noah answered. "Like dolphins. And humpback whales."

"You're a humpback whale," Gianni said to him.

———

December 7, Tuesday

Mom said, "What happened to your mouth?"

I did not want to tattle.

"Your lip looks funny," she said. "Did you bite your lip?"

"No," I said.

"Did Elizabeth try to kiss you too?" she asked.

That made me laugh. "No."

"Because she gave Buckey a fat lip last week when she tried to kiss him, and the nurse called me and . . . oh, my goodness, what am I going to do with that girl?"

"I don't know," I said.

And that is all I told my mom about what happened.

I didn't say one thing about Noah's swinging fist and how it

collided with my just-standing-there mouth after
school waiting for the bus today.

Or about what Montana C. said about
Elizabeth and how she better leave Buckey
alone. Or. Else.

I just went to my room. I wanted to relax on my
bed, but I couldn't because all the stuffties are in a fight
about which one of them is leaking tiny plastic balls on my
covers. And whether that is tragic or disgusting.

So I went out into the hall where Elizabeth was slumping.
"You need to stop kissing kids," I told her.

"That's not what you said before," she snapped back.

"When?" I asked. We were two very cranky kids in one
narrow hallway.

"Last year."

"Elizabeth! No." This was ridiculous. This is exactly why I hate
everybody. "I said you should run after kids, trying to kiss them?"

"No," Elizabeth said, standing up with her fists on her
hips. "But you didn't say I NEED to STOP kissing kids. What
you said is that in life you need only food, water, shelter, and
occasionally an umbrella."

"I never said that," I told her.

"You did so. Last year."

"I hate umbrellas," I said. "So there's no way I—"

"You're afraid of umbrellas."

"Shut up."

"You're not allowed to say *shut up!*"

"So what?"

"Justin! You're also not allowed to say *so what!*"

I shrugged. "I don't care." I was suddenly really, really tired.

"I'm pretty sure *I don't care* is against the rules too, Justin," Elizabeth said, sinking back down onto the floor next to my foot. "If you're not careful, you're gonna end up taking a turn as the bad kid, and I'll be the good one."

I sank down beside her. "Did I really say that, occasionally an umbrella?"

"Yup," she said.

"Sorry," I said, and we leaned against each other for a while.

December 8, Wednesday

The first song we have to sing at the holiday concert is called "Hello, Children."

I don't know what the second song will be called.

Maybe "Good-bye, Everybody, and Please Stop Booing."

December 9, Thursday

In between the songs, we will play "Jingle Bell Rock" on our recorders. We tried it today.

Supposedly.

All our recorder songs sound exactly goosily alike.

In the good news department, Montana C. said the apology note Elizabeth gave to Buckey Monday morning is the second-sweetest thing ever. It is on their fridge held up by their second-best magnet.

"Second-best?" I whispered.

"Shhh," Mr. Leonard said. We were supposed to be BOOOCHing, not whispering about first-graders.

"Uh-huh," Montana C. whispered while Mr. Leonard sharpened a pencil. "Because our best magnet is holding up the sweetest thing ever. The note Elizabeth passed to Buckey yesterday. I made a copy of it last night on my mom's printer. You want to see?"

I did. I nodded instead of saying okay, because how did Mr. Leonard hear none of what Montana C. whispered, only my very quiet question *second-best*?

After making sure Mr. Leonard wasn't looking at us, Montana C. pulled a piece of paper out of her pocket. She silently unfolded it, checked to make sure Mr. Leonard was still stooped over Rozzie Constantine's desk, and plopped it into my book.

I would know Elizabeth's handwriting anywhere. The note looked like this:

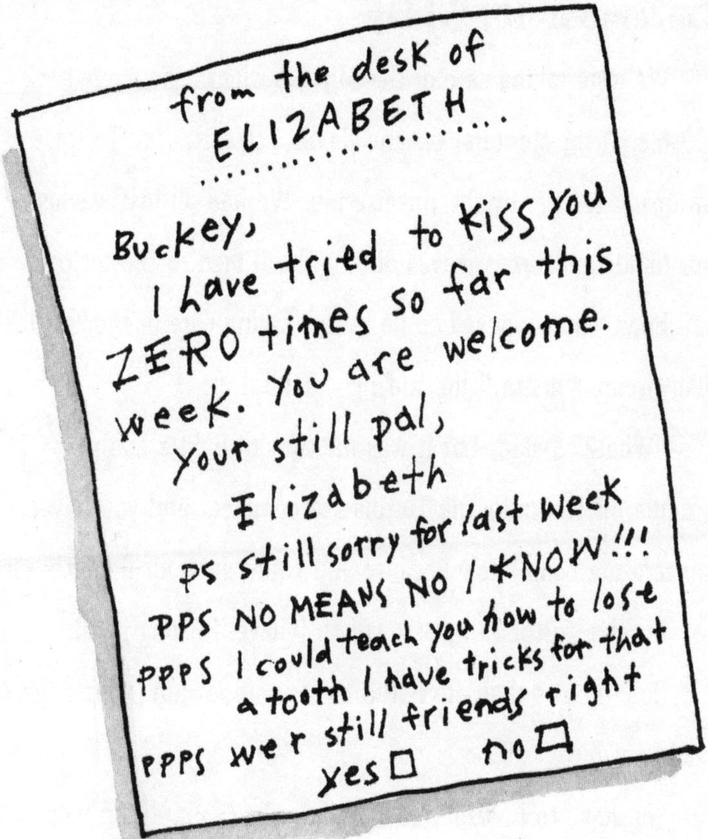
from the desk of
ELIZABETH

Buckey,
I have tried to kiss you
ZERO times so far this
week. You are welcome.
your still pal,
Elizabeth
ps still sorry for last week
PPS NO MEANS NO I *KNOW!!!
PPPS I could teach you how to lose
a tooth I have tricks for that
PPPS wer still friends right
yes ☐ no ☐

December 10, Friday

We were taking care of the tortoise when it happened.

Me, Cash, Montana C., and Xavier Schwartz (the Tortoise Group) were over by the tortoise bin. We had all just washed our hands and taken leaves of arugula to feed to the tortoise.

Noah was supposed to be in the Taking Care of the Tropical Fish Group. "Justin," he said right behind me.

"What?" I said, but it was my turn to hold a leaf of arugula for Lightning the Tortoise to come eat and you have to concentrate completely because you could get your finger bitten off. Russian tortoises have no teeth but very strong jaws.

Noah knows that. He is full of facts about how your fingers could get bitten off.

You have to be especially careful, Mr. Leonard had just reminded us, because Lightning the Tortoise did not get the memo about how tortoises are supposed to be slow. Not when there's arugula involved, that is for sure. Lightning the Tortoise is a BIG fan of arugula.

"Justin!" Noah yelled in my ear. "I am talking to you!"

"Hold on, Noah," I said. "I'm doing something."

"Can't you ever leave Justin alone?" Cash asked him.

"Yeah, Noah," Xavier Schwartz said. "Stop being so annoying all the time, would you?"

"Justin," Noah said, in a growly voice, "if you don't talk to me now, I am going to shoot you with a rubber band."

"Shut up, Noah," I said. Even though you are not allowed to say *shut up*. Not in my family and not in school.

I know it. I know I broke that rule.

And I also know I didn't care.

Lightning the Tortoise chomped away at the piece of arugula I was holding for her. Xavier Schwartz and Montana C. and Cash were all laughing and pointing and saying *How hungry can a little tortoise be?* and *Look, did you see how pink her tongue is?* But I wasn't laughing or pointing or saying things.

I was getting ready to be hit with a rubber band.

Because here are some facts about Noah:

1. He is at least as bad at ball sports as I am, maybe worse

2. He knows millions of facts about fish and diseases

3. He is very kind when you need a friend to just stay by your side because you are having a worried day

4. He has very large hair

But the biggest fact about Noah is:

5. If he says he is going to do something, he is absolutely going to do it.

So when Lightning the Tortoise finished eating the leaf of arugula, I took a big breath. I was very worried about how it was going to feel to be hit with a rubber band because although I am nine years old, almost nine and a half, I have never been shot with one yet in my entire life.

Which Noah, as one of my best friends of my entire life, knows.

In fact, he is probably my best friend even though I always think of him as my second-best. Daisy has always had the slot of my best friend. But really, I think she hasn't really been my best friend for more than a year. I don't know if she is mad at me for something or if an unlisted rule of fourth grade is you can't be best friends with a boy if you are a girl. Or if she just wanted a change. But we haven't had a regular playdate since second grade, back when neither of us had very many teeth. So Noah probably moved up a slot when I wasn't paying attention.

Which probably means Noah is my best friend. He knows that I am actually very scared of many things, including falling off a cliff, food that jiggles, death, bad guys, my dog, umbrellas, getting eaten by a bullhead shark—and getting shot by a rubber band.

And, it turns out, I was right to be scared of at least one of those things, I found out today.

Because when I finished feeding that leaf of arugula to Lightning the Tortoise, I took my deep breath and started to turn around—and one of the things I am most scared of in the whole world hit me in the face.

I saw Noah's hand in the shape of a gun. A rubber band was looped around his pinky, stretched past his thumb onto his pointer finger. With one little twitch of the pinky, he shot the rubber band across the few inches toward my head.

It hit me in the eye.

OW OW OW OW OW.

I am not sure how I ended up on the floor, but Mr. Leonard scooped me up from there and carried me down to the nurse's office. I might have gotten his shirt a little soggy from the eye juice or maybe I was crying.

"It's okay, Justin," he said. "I gotcha."

I rested my head against his white shirt, which was soft and smelled like a pool. He had never called me Justin before. Only *young man*.

I spent the rest of the afternoon waiting in the nurse's office with a bag of blue goo on my eye until my mom could get to school to pick me up. It didn't hurt so terribly much, but still, Mom was already on her way.

I spent a little of my time on the nurse's cot wondering what happened to Noah, if he was sitting in the Principal's Office and if his mom would put him in trouble finally. Which might actually help him, in his personality department.

I spent a lot of my time there thinking about the spelling fact that Dad had taught me, the one about how that word *FRIEND* has the word *END* in it.

And also how the word *NOAH* is made of: *Ah, NO.*

—mm—

December 11, Saturday

This weekend, I guess it's my turn to have parents marching into my room for a talk, and Elizabeth to have Qwerty in her room to wonder together what the heck is going on in the other room.

I am starting to think soccer wasn't the worst way to spend a weekend.

"How's your eye feeling?" Mom asked, frowning at the little mark of bruise next to it.

"Fine. A little too big for the socket, still," I said. "So maybe I can get an eye patch and be a pirate?"

"Justin," Dad said, sitting on the edge of my bed. "What's going on between you and Noah?"

"Nothing," I said.

"You said you would tell us more about what happened in the morning," Mom said. "So. It's morning."

"You'll tell Noah's mother," I argued.

"That's not the issue here, Justin," Dad said.

"Please don't say anything to her, please? Do you promise?"

I waited, looking at Mom.

"Justin," Mom said. "I don't want to promise anything until I hear what really happened. That's not tattling, it's just . . . It's—discussing. That's part of my job, and your job too. We talk about stuff, even tough uncomfortable stuff, in our family, and we figure out how to make things better. Together. So after we talk about what happened, we'll make a decision together about what to do next."

"But what if your decision is to do something I don't want you to do?"

"I promise I'll tell you what I decide to do before I do it," Mom said. "And I'll listen, seriously, to any objections you have. And keep an open mind. Maybe even change my decision. How's that? Fair enough?"

"Fair enough," I said.

"Plus my decision might be just to listen to what's going on with you."

"Yeah," I said. "That might be all you have to do."

She winked at me. "Cool. So?"

"It was no big deal anyway," I told her. "Noah said he was going to shoot me with a rubber band if I didn't talk to him, and I didn't talk to him, so he shot me." I left out the part about me saying *shut up*.

I took out some of my Knights to start a battle to the death.

"Did Noah say he was sorry?" Mom asked.

"No," I said. "He never does."

"This has happened before?"

"Not with a rubber band," I said. Steeltrap stabbed Achilles Heel in the eye with his sword. Achilles Heel fell down in agony.

"But—Noah has hurt you before this?"

I shrugged.

"I thought he was your best friend," Dad said.

"Yeah," I said. "I sort of thought so too."

Mom gathered me up into a hug and said stuff like, *Oh, Justin,* and *Tsk* and *Ugh.* But she knocked over a whole legion of Good Guy Knights with that hug. The Bad Guy Knights started their huge celebration even before Mom and Dad finally left my room.

—*m*—

December 12, Sunday

The lady at the supermarket checkout this morning asked me, "Hey, what happened to your eye?"

I said, "My ex-best friend shot me in it with a rubber band."

On our way to the car, Poopsie said I should answer the next person who asks by saying, "You should see the other guy."

"But the other guy looks fine," I told him. "He needs a haircut, maybe, but . . ."

"So far, he looks fine," Poopsie said. "But just wait 'til Monday when . . ."

"Stop it, you goose," Gingy told him. "Justin, you look very handsome."

"Thanks," I said. "Like a Boss?"

"Like a tough guy who is really a good guy," Gingy added. "Stay that way."

"Okay," I said. "I'm trying."

—————

December 13, Monday

Mom made me a banana-strawberry smoothie AND Cream of Wheat with no lumps. My favorite breakfast.

"Is it my half birthday?" I asked.

"Not yet," Mom said. "I want to talk with you."

I slipped into my seat. She put extra sugar in the Cream of Wheat, then poured milk around the edge, to make a moat for the Sunset of Butter to melt into.

While I stirred, Mom sat down next to me, her coffee cup between her hands.

"Here's what I think you need to say to Noah," Mom said. "Just say, 'Noah, I have asked you not to hit me, kick me, shoot me with rubber bands, or—' "

"I actually never asked him to not shoot me with a rubber band," I interrupted. "He just knows I'm scared of getting shot by a rubber band. But I never actually—"

"Fine," Mom said.

"Am I in trouble?" I asked. Because she seemed pretty mad.

"No," she said, still sounding mad. "Okay. I think actually you can just say, 'Noah, if you hurt me again, I am going to hurt you back.' "

"What?" I put down my spoon. I couldn't believe it. "What happened to Use Your Words Not Your Fists?"

"You will be using your words," Mom said.

"To threaten to use my fists!"

"But—"

"I'd get in big trouble, Mom!"

Her shoulders slumped. She stared into her coffee.

"Plus," I said, "wouldn't it just be wrong? To say I would hurt him, and especially to then actually hurt him? Because, remember? Violence solves nothing. Right?"

"Sure, Gandhi," Mom answered. "But meanwhile, here you sit, my baby, with a black eye, so . . ."

"Gandhi?"

"Never mind."

"Did you just call me Gandhi?"

She sighed.

"My name is Justin."

"I know," Mom said. She kissed my cheek. "You're a good boy, Justin. But here is an important rule. You listening?"

"Yep." I took a sip of the smoothie. It was delicious.

"You are not allowed to let anybody hurt you."

I was still sucking down that smoothie, so I didn't say anything.

"You understand?" Mom asked me. "You are not allowed to let anybody hurt you. It's a rule. A very important rule. Okay?"

"Okay," I said.

I was thinking, as I tied my sneakers, what a weird rule that was, but by the time I got to school, I was thinking the opposite—that it was a pretty good rule to lean on.

But Noah wasn't in school, so I didn't have to make any choices about how to deal with him. Instead me and Xavier Schwartz and Cash and Montana C. talked a lot about tools, and not the kind that Mr. Leonard means, like transition words. The kind that is called *screwdrivers*. And what an awesome, hilarious prank we could do if we make The Screwdriver Club. And how sorry Noah would be if we really do it.

— ⁓⁓ —

December 14, Tuesday

The reason Noah wasn't in school yesterday:

He was suspended for shooting me in the eye with a rubber band.

He had to write me an apology note before he could come back to class 4-L. Mr. Leonard brought the two of us right to the school psychologist's office, even before morning announcements, so Noah could give me the note he wrote at home last night.

I had to read the note right there in front of Noah and the school psychologist. The note said:

Dear Justin,

I am sorry I shot you in the eye with a rubber band. But I am sorry for what you did, too, which is be mean to me and exclude me and bully me all year.

Your friend?

Noah

Then we had to shake hands and say we would try to be better friends.

But what I was actually thinking was:

That was the lousiest apology I ever saw.

—*ww*—

December 15, Wednesday

Mom agreed.

She brought me to school this morning and was waiting there to speak with Noah's mom. When they walked toward 4-L, Mom said to Noah's mom, "May I speak with you please?"

Noah and I walked into the classroom without looking at each other while the moms talked. They have been friends forever too, those moms—just like me and Noah. Before we even got to our desks, the moms were yelling so loudly at each other, they had to be escorted by the hall monitor to the Principal's Office.

Cash whispered to me that he was pretty sure my mom could take Noah's mom in a fight.

I usually hate when my mom is at school, but I liked it when she yelled, "Justin has nothing to apologize for AT ALL!" right before the hall monitor grabbed her by the elbow.

I also liked the idea of her and Noah's mom being put in trouble, sitting sad and sorry, slumped next to each other in the

Bad Kid chairs outside the Principal's Office with Ms. Robitel frowning down at them.

"Do you think they had to shake hands and say they'll try to be better friends?" I asked Noah as we lined up for recess.

"No," Noah said.

Out at recess everybody was crowding around me saying how cool my mom was. "Justin's mom could beat up Mr. Calabrio!" Xavier Schwartz yelled. Unfortunately, Mr. Calabrio was right behind Xavier when he said that.

So Xavier had a nice little sit-down-on-the-cold-grass time while the rest of us tried again with lacrosse and a few of us whispered in between plays about The Screwdriver Club and what to do if we are not allowed to use our dads' tools but we need a screwdriver to be in the club. (Ask for one as a present is the answer everybody agreed on, probably because Cash suggested it.)

December 16, Thursday

Everybody has opinions on how I should act to Noah:

Dad thinks I should take a break from him because he is making unkind choices.

Mom thinks I should tell him he is not allowed to hurt me.

Cash thinks we (The Screwdriver Club) should unscrew all the screws on Noah's chair so when he sits on it, it will collapse and he will fall on the floor and it will be hilarious.

Xavier Schwartz thinks *yeah*.

Montana C. thinks I should give Noah the warning first of *he better leave me alone. Or. Else.* And the *Or. Else* would be The Screwdriver Club plan of unscrewing his chair.

Daisy thinks I should ask Noah why he's being rough lately, because maybe he is having personal troubles. (She is way too nice to be in The Screwdriver Club, obviously. So it is secret from her too.)

Snakey thinks I should bite Noah.

Steeltrap thinks I should jab him with a plastic sword.

Wingnut thinks I should be patient and gentle.

Achilles Heel thinks I should be brave.

Elizabeth thinks I should kiss him, because kissing people makes them run away from you.

Qwerty agrees with everybody.

The only one who has no idea what I should do is me.

―――

December 17, Friday

I sat down next to Noah at the lonely end of the lunch table. I plopped my lunch bag down and climbed onto the bench with Noah watching me, his tuna sandwich blocking the bottom half of his face. His mom makes him huge sandwiches, on a roll instead of plain bread.

"Here's the thing, Noah," I said, without taking out my on-normal-bread sandwich or even my apple slices. "We've been friends for a long time and I want to stay friends." Started with my positive thing.

"You don't act it," Noah said. He took a huge fresh bite of his sandwich.

"Yeah, well," I said, "you don't act it either, like a friend."

"I'm not the one who's being a bully, Justin! You are!"

"Wait," I said. "Stop." I closed my eyes, trying to concentrate, because I had worked very hard on what I was going to say to him. I had listened to the constructive criticisms of all my stuffties and Knights and friends and family members to put together exactly what I wanted to say. I didn't want to mess it up.

"I want to stay friends," I said.

"You already said that."

"Noah." I crumpled my lunch bag a little in my hands. "Okay. I don't want to be mean to you. But the thing is, I am not allowed to let anybody hurt me and you keep hurting me. Maybe you're mad that I'm friends with other kids instead of only you, but too bad because, well, I am friends with them. That's not bullying. It's just being friends."

I opened my eyes. Noah was chewing.

"And I want to be friends with you too," I continued. "But you have to be less annoying and violent. Because being annoying is . . . well, annoying. And violence is never the answer please let me know what you decide the end, thank you."

Then I got up and went to the other end of the table where the friends who had never (so far at least) bruised me up were finishing their lunches. "Why were you even talking to that guy?" Cash asked me.

I shrugged.

"Did you say *Or. Else*?" Montana C. asked.

I shook my head.

"Well, you meant Or. Else, so maybe you kind of said it, just not in words," she suggested. "Right?"

"I don't know," I said. "Maybe."

"Let's go outside," Cash said.

"Yeah," everybody answered. Of course.

Cash tossed his lunch garbage in the trash can and walked out with Montana C. All the other kids in The Screwdriver Club followed them, so I did too.

I didn't get to eat, but it was okay because my heart was too poundy for eating anyway. Noah went to extra recorder practice instead of going outside again.

I know he stinks at recorder, but still, I think that was not a great choice.

December 18, Saturday

Happy Hanukkah. I got some books. Also a screwdriver of my own, just like I asked for. It felt solid, like a weapon, in my hand. My palms started sweating. So I put it down quickly on the table and didn't touch it anymore.

"Don't you like it, Justin?" Dad asked.

"Yes," I said, and got hugged by him. He was proud because he thought I wanted to *build* things with the screwdriver. That made my insides feel like they were made out of extremely bad pie.

Then we had our Hanukkah tradition of setting off the smoke alarm before we went to the diner for dinner because for goodness sake.

―᷍᷍᷍᷍―

December 19, Sunday

Qwerty got a pull toy and a new bone for Hanukkah presents. I didn't even know he was Jewish, or half-Jewish, like me. He looked at me like, *Yeah, well, apparently I am don't touch my stuff.*

I thought about calling Noah on the telephone to ask if he had decided to be less annoying or not yet. And in case I forgot to say it on Friday, maybe even add, *please*. Not as an Or. Else. Not as a threat. Just as a please, like a hope.

But then I didn't call him.

It's my half birthday today. I'm not plain nine anymore. My screwdriver is on top of my desk. I haven't screwed or unscrewed anything with it yet, but it looks like a tool that would work. Really well. Which is a little cool and a little scary.

—————

December 20, Monday

I don't think my Screwdriver Club friends are believing the words to our second song for the Holiday Assembly, which are: "Let us all work for peace, peace, peace / Shalom Salaam Pax Pace Peace Peace Peace. Let us work together for peace."

Too bad we're not singing, *Let us all bring screwdrivers to school tomorrow and see what mischief we can do with them.*

That would be more true.

Tomorrow is the day.

Which is why I am lying here wide awake in the dark while everybody in my family is fast asleep, including the people, the dog, and almost all the stuffties. I am holding my new screwdriver like a Boss.

Or maybe like a Bad Guy.

—mm—

December 21, Tuesday

"We should just go now," Cash said.

"And what?" Montana C. asked.

"And unscrew Noah's chair," Xavier explained.

"Duh," Montana C. said. "But I mean, what, ask Mr. Leonard if we can quickly go to the classroom, the four of us alone?"

"Hmm," Cash said. "No way he'll okay that."

"And even if we could get in there alone right now, will we have enough time?" Montana C. asked. "It's almost time for everybody to go in anyway."

We slumped down onto the cold grass. Three of us were disappointed that maybe our plan wouldn't work. One of us (me) was a little bit relieved. The student council, including Cash as representative of 4-L, had convinced the grown-ups we need free play at least some days of the week. That's why we had time to plot secret evil shenanigans.

Those grown-ups might have been wrong to listen to us, after all.

"I got it," Cash said.

"Great," Xavier said.

"We could say we want to come in early tomorrow morning," Cash suggested. "To, like, do an extra-credit project on tortoises, how about?"

"Yeah!" Xavier said.

"He'd let us," Cash said. "He loves if you want to do extra. Almost as much as he loves coffee. And, oh, this is good. He always has his mug of coffee in the morning when we get there. Right?"

"Yeah," Montana C. said. "So?"

"That means he goes to the teachers' room to *get* the coffee," Cash said, nodding slowly. "So we'd have those few minutes while he's out of the room. If we all work together, we should have all the screws out in a minute, two at most."

"Yeah!" Xavier gave Cash a high five. "This is so awesome!"

"That could work," Montana C said. "But, just . . . It's definitely not mean to do this, right?"

"Definitely not," Cash said. "It's a joke!"

"It's hilarious," Xavier agreed.

Montana C. turned to me. "What do you think, Justin?"

"Well," I said. "It definitely would be funny, but . . ."

"It will be the most awesome thing ever," Xavier yelled.

"Are you kidding me?" Cash asked. "It'll be better than that. Everybody in the school will wish they were in on it. People will probably lie and say they were! But we'll know the truth. It's not mean at all. It's, picture it. It's just, like, pure. Pure funny. It's perfect. We'll have pulled off the perfect—"

"Wow, Cash," Montana C. said. "You want to marry it or what? It's just a prank, right?"

"Yeah," Cash said. "Of course. I was just saying. The perfect prank. Anyway, we already decided."

"Yeah," Xavier yelled.

Cash nodded slowly. "Good thinking, Justin Case."

"Yeah," Montana C. said. "And Mr. Leonard always has a fresh cupful of coffee in the afternoons. So he'll definitely have to go out to get that, and . . ."

"Exactly," Cash said. "Awesome."

"*Kabloingo!*" Xavier yelled. "I don't care when we do it! The sooner the better! But whenever! *Kafloopsie!*" He threw himself up in the air and splattered down near my feet, where he flopped around like a dying Sloane's viperfish.

"I don't . . ." I said, untoppled. "I don't think we should do it."

"You mean, tomorrow morning before school?" Montana C. asked. "Or the after-lunch idea? Because I actually think your tomorrow-after-lunch idea is great."

I took a deep slow breath. "I mean, at all," I said. "I don't think we should unscrew Noah's chair screws."

"But it will be awesome and hilarious!" Xavier yelled. "Best prank EVER!"

"It totally will," Montana C. said. "It's just a joke, Justin Case! Just a funny prank. Right?"

"It'll be so Boss!" Xavier yelled, flinging himself around some more.

"And what else would a Screwdriver Club even do?" Cash asked. "Like, what would be the point of even having a Screwdriver Club?"

"I don't know," I said to my feet.

"We all got screwdrivers," Cash said. "For what?"

"Somebody's chair is getting unscrewed," Xavier Schwartz said, suddenly standing still. "Definitely. Now it's just a question of whose."

They all stared at me.

That is exactly what I was afraid of. As bad as it was down at the lonely end of the table after the Penelope Ann Murphy kerfuffle, how much worse would it be to be the one on the exploded chair, all over the floor?

The answer to that horrible question:

Much worse.

Much, much, much worse.

The way to not be the one on the unscrewed, collapsing chair:

Smile and go along.

Say *just kidding you guys! It was just a joke I was making! Let's do it!*

Maybe I could even not unscrew Noah's screws. I could just stand there and kazoo it—don't do the violence but don't let anybody hurt me, either.

I knew that was the right thing to do. The smart thing. Easiest thing in the world.

But I could not make my voice say, *Yeah! Let's do it!*

Instead my voice said the horrible words of:

"No. Let's not do it."

"You mean you want to quit the club?" Montana C. asked.

"Not really," I mumbled. "I just don't . . ."

"If you quit," Xavier Schwartz said, "you better not tell on us when we unscrew a chair tomorrow, whoever's we unscrew."

"I wouldn't."

"No?" Xavier Schwartz asked, his lips as tight as his fists. "Because sometimes you do tattle, Justin Case."

"Or. Else." Montana C. squinted her eyes at me.

"He won't tell," Cash said. "Come on, you guys."

I wished for myself to say, *Fine, fine, I'm in. Let's do this!* But myself did not say anything.

"You're in or you're out," Cash said. "Come on, Justin Case. Don't worry. We won't get caught."

"That's not . . . that's not the only worry I have of it," I mumbled.

"He has a lot of worries," Xavier Schwartz explained. "He really can't help it."

"It'll be fine," Cash said. He bumped me a little with his side. "We gotta all be in, though. So—okay? Stay late today? Or tomorrow morning early or tomorrow after lunch? Those are our choices."

"I might have to go to the dentist today," Xavier said. "But I'm not sure."

"So lunch tomorrow is good," said Montana C.

"Great," Cash said. "Or how about this: we try coming in early tomorrow morning, and then if we don't get it done, like, if Mr. Leonard skips his coffee or some other kid comes in early and is sitting there like a witness, we still have the come-in-early-from-lunch option."

"Yeah," said Montana C. "Great!"

"Yeah!" yelled Xavier Schwartz.

"No," said me.

Mr. Calabrio blew the whistle. It was time to go back inside.

"No to tomorrow, or no to ever?" Cash was staring at me in a very serious, very hard way. "Last chance, Justin Case," he said. "Are you in?"

Like a Tug-of-War rope, I waggled back and forth, feeling yanked. But then I shook my head and out of my mouth came that word again. "No."

Cash shook his head too. "Then you're out."

He walked away from me. Montana C. and Xavier Schwartz followed him in. I had to walk the long way from the Upper Playground back into school all by myself.

—⁓⁓⁓—

December 22, Wednesday

Dad drove me to school early. "How are things with Noah these days?" he asked on our way.

"Fine," I said. I watched the houses speed backward out of sight and imagined that I had a pet monkey who'd follow us along the drive to school and he would be my best friend. We could hang out together, me and the monkey, at recess.

"Justin?"

"What?"

"I was asking you . . . Never mind. You okay?"

"Mmm-hmm," I said, and I got out of the car because we were at school. I went right up to 4-L, instead of waiting in the lunchroom with the other early kids. But nobody stopped me and asked what I thought I was doing, mister.

Mr. Leonard was in the classroom early, just like Cash had predicted. "Early today, eh, young man?"

I nodded and slumped down in the cozy corner, pretending to read my BOOOCH. I wasn't really concentrating on the story even though it was a good book. I needed to pay attention.

I was there on the rug when Xavier Schwartz and Montana C. came in, a few minutes after Mr. Leonard left to get coffee. Cash came in five seconds later.

None of them said hi to me and I didn't say hi to them, either. They stood there looking around at one another and at me and at the open classroom door. They were all gripping their backpacks very tight.

"Wow," Mr. Leonard said, in the doorway.

All three of them jumped a tiny bit.

"So many early birds this morning," Mr. Leonard said. "Glad I'm not a worm."

None of us laughed.

"Oh, sorry," Mr. Leonard said. "I forgot. You wanted to do extra research on tortoises, right?"

"Yeah," we all lied, and then had to look up tortoise facts together while everybody else came in.

When it was time to get the day started, I put my BOOOCH on my desk and I sat down.

My chair collapsed under me. I crashed onto the floor in a heap of chair pieces and clatter and me.

Kaplooie.

December 23, Thursday

"I didn't do it," Cash said for the billionth time. "I swear."

"I believe you," I said, also for the billionth. Ever since my chair collapsed, those guys weren't ignoring me anymore. So that was a plus, at least. We were sitting in the backstage area, waiting for the third-graders to finish rehearsing their dance before it was our turn to practice.

"So who did unscrew Justin Case's chair?" Xavier whispered, even though it was Ms. Zhang in charge of us and she didn't care if we talked. "Somebody must have stayed late after school yesterday, right?"

"Definitely," Montana C. said. "But who?"

"Well, it had to be one of us," Xavier whispered. "Because, who else?"

"Obviously." Montana C.'s eyes flicked over to Cash, then away.

"I didn't do it," Cash said for the billion and oneth time.

"Well, I didn't do it," Montana C. said.

"Me neither," Xavier whispered. "Do you think Mr. Leonard has figured out who did it yet?"

Mr. Leonard had spoken to each of us privately, one at a time, during recess after lunch and all through the afternoon while Ms. Robitel from the office watched the rest of us pretend to read our BOOOCHes. The custodian brought me a spare chair from class 4-T to sit on when I wasn't the one being asked questions by Mr. Leonard. After me, he called Cash in to talk with him, and then Montana C. Everybody looked down at their BOOOCHes while the kid whose name got called walked across the front of the classroom and out to the hall with Mr. Leonard.

"He sure is talking to Noah for a long time," Montana C. whispered. "Didn't he talk to Noah yesterday?"

"Yup," I said.

"Hey," Cash said. "Do you think Noah somehow found out about our plan?"

"You think *Noah* is the one who stayed late yesterday afternoon and unscrewed Justin Case's chair as revenge?" Xavier asked.

"Pre-revenge, you mean," Montana C. said. "Because we didn't . . . you know, and Justin didn't even want to unscrew Noah's, so why would Noah—"

Xavier interrupted, "Does Noah even have a screwdriver?"

"*Beep boop beep,*" Gianni Schicci said, pretending to be a robot. "*Beep beep boop boop beep.*"

The third-graders finished, so we all started getting up.

"What exactly happened?" Daisy asked. "I don't get why your chair just—collapsed like that."

"It lost all its screws," I said. "Somehow."

She laughed a little. "Just—lost its screws?"

"How could that happen?" Rozzie Constantine asked. "One screw loose, sure, but . . ."

"Somebody obviously stayed after school Tuesday to unscrew them," Xavier Schwartz said.

Daisy gasped. "Why would somebody *do* that?"

"I know it wasn't me," Xavier answered. "Because I would have seen me there. And I didn't."

"Also you had a dentist's appointment," Montana C. said.

"Turns out, I didn't," he said.

"Aha!" Cash yelled, pointing at Xavier.

"Fourth-graders, please take your spots on the risers," Ms. Zhang said.

"Justin's arms were all up in the air like this," Bartholomew Wiggins said, walking past us with his arms above his head.

Cash tipped his head and squinted at Bartholomew Wiggins.

"Nah," Montana C. whispered. "No way."

"Quiet, please," Mr. Leonard said, loping down the auditorium aisle with Noah trudging behind him. "Sorry for the delay. Let's all get to our proper places now. This is our last run-through before the concert tomorrow."

I heard Gianni grumble to Xavier, "Can't believe I have to be in the other class and miss everything good."

"Best prank ever," Xavier Schwartz whispered back. "Whoever did it is a genius."

"Young man!" Mr. Leonard said, with one eyebrow up in Xavier Schwartz's direction. Then we all sang again about how much we wanted peace, peace, peace.

On our way back to 4-L in one silent line, Noah whispered to me, "I bet you anything Cash did that to you, the prank with your chair collapsing. And I told Mr. Leonard all my theories about it."

I just shrugged, partly because we were supposed to be silent as sharks.

December 24, Friday

At the Holiday Concert, the first-graders were supposed to throw their paper snowflakes into the audience of parents and teachers and other kids at the end of their song "No School Cuz It Snowed."

But most of them wanted to keep their snowflakes. There was a whole kerfuffle about it, with the teachers yelling, "Throw them!" and the kids yelling back, "No!" and "I'm keeping mine!"

Elizabeth yelled the loudest.

Fourth grade was second to last, right before the kindergartners. We sang pretty okay, I think, and some of the kids in our grade had actually learned how to play their recorders. Not me. Kazooed it the whole way through.

At lunch Noah sat down next to me. Before he even unwrapped his hugie sandwich, he picked up an Oreo. "Want it?" he asked me.

"But you only have three," I said.

He shrugged and held it out to me. I took it. "Thanks, Noah," I said.

I ate it before I took out any of my own lunch. I had just unwrapped my sandwich when Cash said, "Let's go," to me. It's lucky I was full of cookie.

On our way to the playground, Xavier Schwartz asked me, "So, Noah's your buddy again?"

I shrugged. "Sure."

"Yeah, true," Xavier Schwartz said. "Gianni Schicci is my best friend, and he thinks he's a robot."

"What are you gonna do?" Cash asked.

"Yeah," Montana C. said, throwing her arms across my shoulders and Cash's. "What are you gonna do?"

Cash's cheeks turned a little pink.

And then, even weirder than that, when we got in, we had no math test, no spelling test—just a dance party, with cookies Mr. Leonard made himself. All afternoon until 3:10, when we all said the hilarious joke of "See you next year" to each other and packed up our stuff because it was the best word: *VACATION.*

—⟶—

December 25, Saturday

Elizabeth and I woke up early and tried to guess what was in all those packages. We started with pretty good guesses, but after a few minutes we were guessing that small rectangular book-shaped packages were camels and watermelons.

"First grade is more complicated than I expected," she whispered.

"Wait 'til fourth grade," I whispered back.

"I sure hope one of these things is a time machine," she said. "Because sometimes I want to be in some other when than now."

"Seriously," I agreed.

After present-opening, we had a full-family wrapping-paper fight, with wrapping-paper snowballs. Qwerty won. Then Elizabeth and I got started on building our own time machine with the art supplies we both got.

December 26, Sunday

It was so quiet when I woke up, I thought it was still night. But no, it was way too bright in my room. *Maybe the world ended,* I thought. Or maybe the time machine worked and I was transported to some other when, all alone.

Tiptoeing downstairs, I realized that, more likely, I was just the first in our family to wake up. I was getting happy about that idea because then I could sneak over to the no-money-required gum-ball machine we got as a family gift and have as many gum balls as I wanted, and work on my awesome gum-chewing skills.

But no all to those ideas.

Mom was standing at the back door, holding her coffee mug, looking out into the yard, where everything was glittery white. The snow was falling in fist-size flakes.

I stood next to her and watched too. First snow of the whole year.

She put her arm around me, so I leaned against her. She didn't ask, *How's everything going?* or *Did anything weird happen at school this week?* We just stood there in the quiet and watched the snow come down, together.

Soon Dad and Qwerty came back from their walk, and Elizabeth came down from her room where she had built an awesome ninja princess fort addition for our time machine.

After some cleaning up of the very gluey ninja princess fort addition, and breakfast of waffles made on Dad's new waffle iron, we all went outside. We had a snowball fight with actual snow and screaming and runny noses and freezing toes. But the silvery quiet of the morning, when just Mom and I stood there alone together, stayed inside me the whole day.

All the way until night, when I heard the plan for New Year's Eve.

—_wm_—

December 27, Monday

"But why do we have to go?" I asked.

"Oh, Justin," Mom said. "I thought you liked Cash."

"I do," I said. "But . . ."

"And they're new in town, and trying to connect with people. It's nice that they're having a New Year's Eve party. A lot of kids you know will be there, I'm sure. Please, no more complaining."

"I wasn't . . ."

"Cash's mom told me that he is in The Screwdriver Club with you. I didn't know you were in The Screwdriver Club!"

My mouth opened and closed a few times without making sounds.

"I actually never heard of a screwdriver club. Is that a new thing at school this year?"

"I—I—I guess."

"Well, I told her Cash could come over tomorrow and bring his new screwdriver so you guys can . . . What do you do with screwdrivers in your club?"

"Nothing."

"Nothing? Wow, sounds like a fun club!" She winked at me. What did that even mean, that wink? Then she said, "Well, at least it's not just screen time. Do you construct things? Or make models, or what?"

"It's not . . . We don't . . . We do . . . just usual screwdriver type things, I guess," I said. "Nothing too—"

Then there was a splattering crash in the kitchen.

"Elizabeth!" Mom shouted. "How many times do I have to tell you eggs are not for juggling?" Mom ran toward the kitchen, away from me and any more questions about screwdrivers or clubs.

This vacation is really making me appreciate Elizabeth.

—*wwv*—

December 28, Tuesday

Cash sat down behind the wall of the snow fort we were building and wiped his nose on his mitten. "I don't get it," he said.

All the snowballs were next to him. If he decided to go to battle against me, back there behind our shared fort wall in my backyard, I was in deep trouble. He had all the ammo and I had none, and no defense. I should never have admitted the truth to him back there. But it was too late.

I stood here and made a snowball while I repeated what I had just said: "I know you weren't the one who took the screws out of my chair because I'm the one who did it."

"No," Cash said. "I heard you. I just don't get why you took the screws out of your own chair. Did you get confused and think you were doing Noah's? Or, but you said you didn't want to do that. So—why?"

"I *didn't* want to," I said. "Noah's not a bad kid, even if he sometimes acts like it. Like shooting me with a rubber band. That stunk."

"Yeah," Cash said.

"And he's weird sometimes. I admit that for sure."

"So . . ."

"But he's also nice and loyal, and he knows a lot about diseases."

"And fish."

"Yeah," I said. "But he's the kind of kid who, if we took the screws out of his chair and he fell, it would be hilarious to everybody except him. He would be really sad and mad and, like, would feel just terrible."

"But that doesn't . . ." He picked up a snowball and patted it tighter with his mitten paws. "We were getting back at him *for you*, Justin Case."

I put my first snowball down and started on a second. "Right, well. I appreciate that. Seriously. And I was thinking you were right. Not just the revenge thing, though that too, definitely. But also that taking all the screws out of a chair would be an excellent prank. And how funny it would be to see somebody splatter all over the floor when their chair collapses."

"Yeah, so—"

"And I knew we couldn't just not do it. It was too excellent—it had to happen. And so, I . . . I don't know. I'm not saying you'd definitely do it to me if I didn't do it to myself first."

"We might have," Cash said. "You or Noah. Probably Noah. We were still deciding. But I don't know if we ever really would've been able to get it done."

"You would've," I said.

"Thanks," Cash said. "You beat us to it."

"Yeah," I said. "It doesn't make a lot of sense, I guess, but I thought maybe if it happened to me, there'd be a kerfuffle, and—"

"There sure was."

"Yeah," I said. "And, well, I thought that would keep it from happening to Noah."

"It did," Cash said. "It makes sense. You took the hit for Noah. Like a Boss."

I shrugged. "We've been friends a long time."

"That's pretty cool."

"Yeah?"

"Yeah. And you told Mr. Leonard what happened?"

"Well, yeah. I gave him the screws."

"That must've been The Bomb!" Cash said. "Just plunked them onto the table?"

"Yeah," I said. "It was kind of funny. They were rolling off. . . ."

"That is awesome." Cash shook his head. "You told on yourself."

"I didn't want anybody else to get in trouble for it. I thought I was going to get suspended, but he said he couldn't really suspend me for bullying myself, could he? But the next kid who brings a screwdriver to school will be suspended for two days and it will go on our permanent record. So I promised we wouldn't bring them anymore. Which is kind of why I had to tell you about the whole thing."

"Yeah, okay." Cash leaned back against the wall of our fort. "It's funny how Xavier says you are such a worried kid, but you're actually so not."

"Oh," I said. "I so am."

"Nope. You're not."

"Trust me," I said.

"How can I trust you when you pull a secret prank like that?" Cash asked.

"Fair enough," I said. "But—"

"Oh, no! The aliens!" Cash flipped around and pointed across my empty, snowy backyard. "They're attacking!"

"Yeah!" I yelled, and then we used up all our snowballs not on each other but against the invisible aliens that we

pretended had invaded my backyard. After that we went inside and Dad made us hot chocolate. Cash said it was the best "cocoa" he ever tasted in his entire life. Dad gave us extra marshmallows for that.

When we finished our second helping of "cocoa" plus two chocolate-covered graham crackers each, we went up to my room and played with everything at once.

—*m*—

December 29, Wednesday

Report cards came in the mail today. Mom and Dad had some talking to do with each of us, privately. While they were in Elizabeth's room, I set up all my Knights on the floor and all my stuffties on my bed, in neat rows, facing out. They might not all agree with every one of my choices, but they are all on my side and ready to defend me. I finished the battle setup just in time.

Dad sat on my desk chair. Mom sat next to me on the floor. I knew the thing they wanted to talk with me about was not any of the grades or most of the comments because I got even more Exceeding Expectations than Meeting Expectations and zero of either Progressing to Meeting or Area of Concern. I don't know what Elizabeth got because in our family we keep report cards private.

But there was something in the Teacher Comment section I knew they would give me a Talk about and that was:

Why did I take the screws out of my chair last week.

I shrugged.

"That is not an answer, Justin," Mom said.

I took a deep slow breath like Mom always says I should do when I feel worried or stressed. *Slow it down*, she always says.

"Justin, we're waiting," Dad said.

"I know," I said, and took another deep slow breath. "Well, The Screwdriver Club was definitely going to do unscrew somebody's chair, and Noah was the first choice. Because he rubber-band-shot me. So, revenge. But I didn't want them to do that."

"How come?" Dad asked.

"Because he'd be sad. Really sad if that happened to him. You know what I mean?"

Mom put her fingers in front of her mouth but didn't say anything.

It felt kind of good to talk about it. My Knights, all lined up neatly for battle, and my stuffties, all ready to jump in and fight for me too—they all leaned in to listen to the story I was telling instead of gearing up for fighting.

"And there's more," I told everybody.

"Go on," Mom said.

"It's not just that I wanted to protect Noah from the sadness. Which I did, I swear. But also, well, I thought if we did it to Noah, he would tattle on us. And we would all get put in trouble. Which I didn't want. Of course. So I thought maybe I could just unscrew my chair and I would think it was kind of funny even if it was a little scary, so nobody would have to be put in trouble. And then, also, as a bonus, Mr. Leonard would be so busy solving that crime, nobody would be able to unscrew Noah's chair! So it would, like, protect him. But also us."

Everybody just looked at me. Snakey and some of the Knights looked a little not impressed.

"So you *did* unscrew your own chair?" Dad asked. "That was true?"

"Yeah."

"You weren't just saying you did it?" Mom asked. "To cover for somebody else or to avoid being a tattletale?"

"No," I said. "I did it. With my new screwdriver." I wasn't sure if I would be put in more or less trouble for if I lied, but I decided on a what-the-heck-just-tell-the-truth plan because otherwise I would probably get all confused.

"That must have taken a lot of work," Dad said.

"It did." That impressed all the Knights, and Really Giraffe. They are hard workers.

"Were the screws in tight?" Dad asked.

"Some of them," I told him. "The one holding together the back right leg was really . . ."

"I *don't* think *that* is the point," Mom said.

Dad and I looked at our squiggly fingers in our laps.

"Of course not," Dad said quietly. "I was just—"

"The point," Mom interrupted, "Justin, is that we are concerned that you would choose to hurt yourself to cope with a social situation."

"I was getting to that point," Dad mumbled. "Exactly."

"Justin," Mom said. "You are not allowed to hurt *yourself*, either."

"Okay," I said. "I didn't, though."

"Hurt yourself?"

"Yes. I mean, no. I didn't. I mean, I startled myself, even though I was pretty sure my chair would collapse, since all its screws were jangling around in my pocket and the only thing holding it up was, like, habit."

Mom smiled a little but quickly tucked that thing away. I saw it though.

"But I didn't get hurt," I said. "And I was right, about that I would think it was kind of funny instead of sad. It was funny. I was like *kaplooie* all over the floor. And nobody unscrewed Noah's chair by going in early from lunch. So—"

"It was dangerous," Dad said. "You didn't get hurt, but you could have, and you're also not allowed to destroy school property."

"I didn't," I said. "I gave all the screws back to Mr. Leonard. The chair was good as new by the next day."

"Well," Mom said. "It's still not okay."

"I know."

Dad leaned forward. "And you know that if you unscrew anything else at school or even bring your screwdriver to school, you'll be in huge trouble, right?"

"Yeah," I said. "I know. I get it. I really do."

"You don't have to hurt yourself," Mom said. "Or be the class clown to get out of a sticky situation. And, Justin, seriously: You aren't allowed to just go around taking screws out of stuff."

"No matter how funny you think it might be," Dad added.

"Am I punished?" I asked, instead of *Do you think it was funny?*

"Slightly," Dad answered. I think to the question I asked out loud.

My punishment was: I had to go around the house with Dad, both of us with our screwdrivers, and check every screw in the house for looseness. Then tighten anything up that needs it. I agreed that was completely fair. Mom gave me hugs and said they want me to be productive instead of destructive.

It was the best punishment ever. Dad and I tightened *everything*.

Elizabeth is outside, shoveling the walk. I cannot figure out what she did wrong in first grade to get that one.

December 30, Thursday

Second-to-last day of this year.

Gingy and Poopsie came over to stay with us while Mom and Dad worked. We played trick-or-treat, taking turns being the getters and the givers. Poopsie was the best giver. He gave stuff like a pot holder and three cans of tuna and half the blender (bottom half).

Later, while he was reading to Elizabeth, I told Gingy a little bit about The Screwdriver Club and all that. She nodded the whole time I was telling her about it and then said, "Well, I expect everybody told you a bunch of rules about what to do and what not to, since then?"

"Yup," I said. "They sure did."

"And everybody's been droning on and on, I expect, about the fact that teasing somebody about a strength is fine, but teasing somebody who feels weak or vulnerable is just mean. Right?"

"Um," I said. "Not really, no. But I kind of know that, I think."

"I know you do, my darling," Gingy said. "So, that leaves me to tell you about doorknobs, I guess."

And she did.

Things I Am Good at Getting:

4. Crazy ideas

5. Good grandparents

⸻

December 31, Friday

We got Noah to teach us how to shoot rubber bands. Daisy made a target on the back of our Nine Men's Morris game board and we hung it on the back of Cash's closed door. "Too bad we don't have an ax to throw at it," Cash said.

"Yeah," I said. "We could explode a can of soda!"

"That would be awesome!" Xavier said.

"That would be *dangerous*," Noah said. "Do you know how many people die each year from thrown axes?"

"How many?" Cash asked, his hands in his pockets.

I looked at Noah, whose eyes flicked up at mine. I shook my head just a little, just enough for only Noah to see.

"No idea, actually," Noah said. "But probably more than die from rubber-band-target shootings."

"Depends on the year, probably," Cash said.

"Yeah," Xavier said.

"Yeah," said Noah. "Probably."

"When my grandmother was little, she took her dad's screwdriver and unscrewed her doorknob," I said.

Everybody just stared at me.

"She told me about it yesterday," I explained.

"She unscrewed her own doorknob?" Noah asked. "Why would she do a thing like that? And which grandmother, Ninny or Gingy? Those are what Justin calls his grandmothers."

"Gingy," I said. "She just did it to see what would happen."

"And what happened?" Daisy asked.

"Well," I said. "She sat in her room for a long time, waiting, until her father came to get her. She had put the doorknob back in the slot, you know, just no screws. Her dad turned the doorknob and out it plopped. Right onto the floor."

"Seriously?" Cash asked. "Your grandmother is awesome!"

"Everybody in her family was, like, *How in the world did that doorknob just fall off like that?* But she never told anybody she had done it herself until yesterday, when she told me."

"That. Is. Great," Montana C. said. "When I grow up, I want to be Gingy."

"Me too," said Xavier. "Gingy is The Bomb."

"Let's do it," Cash said. "Let's take off my doorknob and see what happens."

We all said *yeah* and got to work. Everybody got a turn with Cash's new screwdriver. Even Noah, who only told everybody how to use it a little. After the screwless doorknob was back in the hole, we just sat around Cash's room waiting, trying not to laugh. It was hard.

Eventually his sisters came and knocked on the door to tell us to come down for dessert. We all clamped our hands over our mouths.

"Y'all in there?" one of the sisters asked.

We watched the doorknob twist. Then clank clank clank went the inside bulb of the doorknob, into Cash's room and across his floor.

We all laughed so hard, eye goo streamed down our faces. "What happened?" one of the sisters asked us. She was bending down so we could see one of her eyeballs through the hole where the doorknob wasn't.

"The Screwdriver Club strikes again!" Xavier Schwartz yelled.

"Suit yourselves," a Cash's sister said. "More cake for us!"

Using Cash's screwdriver, we managed to get out of there and down for cake pretty quickly. Good thing we have excellent tools skills.

And good thing also there was no pie but a lot of cake. Enough for everybody, at least two servings each.

Thank you for reading
this FEIWEL AND FRIENDS book.
The Friends who made

JUSTIN CASE
Rules, Tools,
and Maybe a Bully

possible are:

Jean Feiwel, Publisher

Liz Szabla, Editor in Chief

Rich Deas, Senior Creative Director

Holly West, Associate Editor

Dave Barrett, Executive Managing Editor

Nicole Liebowitz Moulaison, Production Manager

Lauren A. Burniac, Editor

Anna Roberto, Associate Editor

Christine Barcellona, Administrative Assistant

Follow us on Facebook or visit us online at mackids.com.

Our books are friends for life.